# FROM SEOUL WITH LOVE

# From Seoul With Love

## Crystal Symone

The Limitless Pen

From Seoul With Love
A Novel
**Crystal Symone**

Editing, layout & cover design: *Your Writing Table* (www.yourwritingtable.com)

Dedication

This is dedicated to all the women that thought what they needed was their whole life figured out before they turned twenty-five. It's also dedicated to the women that have had to heal from the trauma of their choices. But most importantly this book is a dedication to every woman that finds pleasure in escaping in a good book.

**Thanks to the Ultimate High for blessing me with this gift and for placing a story in my heart.**

Table of Contents

# Prologue

*Every girl has something they regret and would kill to keep from seeing the light of day. My story started long ago and since then I've been trying to make up for the choices I made. But you can't always do the right thing, no matter how much I wish I could go back, I can't. Although the years have passed as I presently look in the mirror, I still see the same girl staring back at me. My 5'8 tall frame slim, chocolate-kissed skin, my doe doe-shaped eyes making me appear to be innocent. Even at the age of twenty-six, my body is that of a woman, but my heart is still that of a girl. Not just any girl but the one who got an abortion at seventeen.*

*If there's anyone up there who listens to a person like me, it's safe to say they've gone quiet since this very instant.*

*A few years ago...*

*"I told her fast ass about going around acting like she's grown, girl I don't know what we gone do. She's been around that no-good Jackson... yeah, the one on the basketball team. I can't let anyone find out she's already showing some in her belly. I can't tell how far along... but a mother knows, and she's been trying to hide herself wearing big sweatshirts and baggy clothes. Harold has enough on his plate with him being deployed in Iraq, I'm going to handle this one on my own can't have him being stressed out there.*

*I overhear my mom talking to someone on the phone. The way her feet pace our checkered black and white tile floor I'm surprised she hasn't* burst a blood vessel or stomped a hole into the floor. Her normal butterscotch skin and signature pink lip are scrunched up in the angriest manner. The hair she pressed three days ago seems to look kinky at the root as sweat and tears stream down her face of frustration. Our house phone hangs on the wall next to the calendar my mom keeps of appointments and birthdays, and when my dad is scheduled to call us, the cord hangs in the air like my voice or lack of one.

She just found out that I'm pregnant by Jackson Hall, my ex-boyfriend, and the star athlete of Williamson High School. It turns out my stomach wasn't getting big because of endless after-school trips to the Taco Bell ten minutes away from my house and even closer to Jackson and his mom's small two-bedroom apartment. How did I get here? After six months of dating, Jackson convinced me that he was ready to know what it felt like to be a real man, and that to prove my love to him I would agree to make love to him. It was a normal Thursday afternoon. I had just finished studying for my calculus test and he had just finished reviewing some basketball plays for his game on Friday against Olympic High. We sat in his small room on the twin bed mattress with blue plaid sheets and a matching comforter. His wall was lined with posters of basketball stars Michael Jordan, Kobe Bryant, and his all-time favorite player Larry Bird. My legs were crossed on his bed, and he was lying down opposite of me. We had spent plenty of afternoons like this on account of his mom always being at work day and night, we always had the place to ourselves. He tells me it's time we take our relationship to the next level and explains that since we love each other we need to express it.

I remember lying on my back softly while Jackson touched the skin on the back of my neck and held my head in place to kiss me. I remember him whispering in my ear that having sex would take our relationship to a whole new level and only increase our love for one another. I remember asking him if we needed a condom and he assured me that since this was our first time, we didn't need one. I remember the way he slid into me, it hurt but wanting *to please him I acted like it felt good. Instead of focusing on the pain coming from between my legs as he pumped away, I stared ever so silently at the post of Michael Jordan hanging next to the computer desk and door. I focused on the way his shoelaces were swinging in the air as he dunked the basketball into the hoop. The way sweat beads formed on his forehead and the way his tongue snuck out of his mouth while this shot was captured. I remember the air smelled of lasagna that Jackson's mother cooked for him before she left for work that day. But most of all I remember feeling like I'd become elevated like this man would be mine and mine only because I gave him something special, the most special thing a 17-year-old girl could give a 17-year-old boy.*

*That afternoon replays like a VHS tape in my head over, and over, and over again. It's been almost three and a half months since Jackson called me and even acknowledged me. I know he's been busy with it being summer and he's been at basketball camp. But that's no excuse they have phones in Orlando, FL where his camp is. The summer is almost over and staring at my body in the downstairs bathroom adjacent to the kitchen my mother keeps pacing, keeps talking, and keeps avoiding my eyes. I look back in the mirror in awe of my belly and the way it hangs over my gray shorts and hoodie lifted over my shoulder exposing what I've been wanting to hide. At first, I thought I was just gaining weight, and since I've never had regular period cycles since I started having a period at the age of twelve. But now looking in astoundment it's clear I was in denial, staring at the rose wallpaper against the bathroom wall I think of a place far away from here. A place where my mind can take me, but my body can't follow a place where there is no judgment, no decisions, and most importantly a place where my choice matters. But instead of a fantasy I hear through the half-open door a reminder that there's no escaping this.*

*My mother talks as if I'm not even here. Every hurtful sentence about how I should be ashamed of myself you couldn't even tell this is the woman that I came out of, it's more like I'm just a girl off the street. Instead of being comforted, I am feeling like a prisoner to this conversation, this decision, and this house.*

*"Well, she's not keeping it," I hear my mom say loud enough for the whole house to hear. Even though it's only me and my mother presently there, that doesn't stop her from repeating herself. I walk back towards the kitchen sitting down at our window kitchen nook and looking at the trees in our backyard, escaping now seems unlikely. She explains to whoever is on the phone that she can't have her reputation or this family's reputation ruined because of a mistake.*

*It isn't enough that we're one of the few black families in the neighborhood in a two-parent household. My mom doesn't care that up until this point, I've been her perfect little scholar and social butterfly being the token black girl in my high school. I don't get an ounce of credit for being brave enough to tell her I'm pregnant. There is no empathy in her voice as I hear her last few statements.*

*"I'm not raising my girls to be nobody's baby momma; she's got plenty of time later in her life to be a mother, but at seventeen she's not ready. Hell, I wasn't, and I'll be damned if she makes the same mistakes I did. The decision is final. I've made the appointment and we're driving across the border, so we won't see anybody we know. I can't risk anyone finding out about this once it's done."*

*My heart plummets and suddenly my decision, my choice, my body has been taken away from me and instead is being controlled by my mother. On that day in August, I rode for five hours in the back seat of my mother's red Ford Escort. The car was deathly quiet between my mother and me the only sound could be heard was a gospel song with a female vocalist belting about God's forgiveness. Even though I was seventeen and old enough to sit in the passenger seat I sat in the back. Soaking up the way my mother's hair looked oddly dull even though she kept her hair pressed and greased. The way her brown eyes would avoid mine as she kept trying to glance at me through the rearview mirror. As we drove through a rural part of South Carolina toward the Tennessee state border I couldn't help but see visions of myself stopping this from happening. One solution is to act violently ill like I'm having a seizure so my mom can pull over and is forced to get out of the car. Then I can climb to the front seat and take off with her left standing confused in the middle of nowhere. I debate if applying my theatre class tactics could work but then remember I can't drive a stick shift car. I don't know why but I just go along with her plan. Once we make it to the border my mom pulls out a small map at the first rest stop, she finds. I am still absently looking out the window watching as a couple pulls off in a blue Mustang, blue like the jersey Jackson wears on game day for our team, The Falcons. She compares the address she wrote down on a piece of paper to the map, our destination: Planned Parenthood.*

*She parks the car in a small corner spot not far from the entrance of the building. Surprisingly she says nothing, only motioning for me to get out of the car and follow her lead. I oblige like a good girl but take what little power I have and use it to hold my head up high. My chest sticking out and my bulbous nose leading the way I shut the door softly as my mother just stares at me over the hood of her car. My fingers move fast playing with the string on my hoodie in eighty-five-degree weather. As we walk towards the doors that seem like the entrance to hell, she tells me to hurry up, and looking to my left I can tell why. On the left side of the parking lot inches away from the curb is a white lady with overalls, and curled blonde bangs, she's holding up a sign. I squint my eyes trying to make out what the sign says, "God made the seed so you don't have to bleed". I'm not sure what the saying means but the lady stares across the parking lot defiantly, she doesn't even attempt to stand up from the plastic folding chair she sits on. Instead, her eyes do the talking, and they are like razorblades to me.*

*My mother hurriedly opens the door of the building and I feel cool air conditioning greeting me. On a hot day like this one that should bring me comfort but instead, it's a reminder of how cold my heart will be after this.*

*My mother takes the lead, a position she's very familiar with and walks to the front desk checking us in for the appointment. I sit down still trying to make an escape plan and feeling like this is my last chance to take control. Unlike the woman sitting across from me with a gold band on her left finger and a bulging belly, I can't quite match her smile as she looks up from a magazine. She's ready to be a mother, but I'm just not.*

*My name is called not long after sitting down but instead of getting up I just sit there even if it's a silent protest it's a protest. It isn't until my mother says my name loud enough to hear over my heart beating that I look up. She and a nurse dressed in pink scrubs, a messy bun, and crooked teeth wait for me with the door halfway open. I'm led to the room where it will happen life will be literally sucked out of me. Or at least that's what it said would happen online. The nurse instructs me to get changed on the bed is a medical gown, the room is an upbeat yellow and pictures line the walls about different birth control pills being advertised. I undress slowly looking at my mother sitting in the corner on a small chair biting her nails in nervousness. I'm not sure why she's nervous, it's me that's about to do something unforgettable, unimaginable not her.*

*The time it takes for the nurse to come back in the room with a doctor seems like five minutes instead of twenty. He walks in not even smiling or bothering to look in my eyes. They seem to be focused on my mother as he explains the process and tells me what to do. First, he hands me some pills that will help with the pain that will come. In the span of ten minutes, he told me that I'll get to hear the baby's heartbeat but after that the procedure will start. Laying back on the bed and putting these weird metal footholds in place my body eases into discomfort. Whether from drugs or disassociation I feel my body start to float. It's like if I think about it hard enough, I can float far away from here... Far away in some place where I never had sex. Some place where I could just run away from my own self and never come back.*

*My body continues to float, and I see the machine being pushed from the edge of the room. I forgot its name, but I know this is to hear the baby's heart. They rub some gel onto my stomach and the slight bulge somehow feels bigger and more pronounced. As the device is turned on a computer monitor comes to life blank at first...but then I see it. I see my baby looking to my mother silently pleading with her to stop forcing me to make this decision. But being the coward, she is her back turns, and she can't stand the sight of me or this baby. Her disappointment, anguish, and hatred sound louder than the ferocious soundtrack of the heartbeat filling the room.*

*Unlike that day I am willing to skip past this and go right to where I am presently. I've heard when something traumatic happens to you your mind can forget but your body always remembers. I guess that's why my womb has never been quite the same nor my relationships. All of them seem to splinter like the weight of this secret only me and my mother hold.*

*When I look in the mirror, I see the same girl that got her choices taken away. If God were listening, I don't think He heard my cry on a hot, sticky sunny day in August otherwise this story would be different and not a familiar march to decisions of the past.*

# Chapter 1

My eyes are closed with my eye mask blocking all sunlight shining through my windows, just as I toss my head on the cool pillow beside me my alarm blares. Since basic training in the Air Force, I wake up at seven a.m. before work and prepare for my two-mile run at Hines Park. Feeling drowsy I turn on my workout playlist to help me get out of bed, adjusting my eyes to the incoming light. Slowly leaning up, I set my feet into my blue house slippers and make my way to the large walk-in closet. Although I've lived in my condo for years my closet looks bare. Another result of being in the military, you learn to pack light. Just as I settle on my Victoria's Secret tights and sports bra, I trip on something on the floor.

*What the hell was that?*

My hands instantly wrap around my Rose sex toy.

*Damn, I left this out,* I laugh in my empty apartment. Just looking at it makes me second-guess my workout plan. Seeing as how I haven't had sex in over two years. Even though the sex toy is obsolete compared to having a real man the plastic can't break my heart unless it's not charged. With one touch of my finger, I feel the toy come to life pulsating like it's ready for me.

Just as I was considering canceling my run, I hear my phone ringing. *Shit.*

Grabbing my phone off the nightstand, I see a familiar name "Incoming call from Drea."

Her contact photo from our graduation day of advanced training both of us smiling with happy glows on our faces. The last time I spoke with her was about Lawrence and it did not end well. I was so fucked up and felt like I couldn't trust anyone including her. Letting the call go to voicemail I see that she left me a message. Either from regret or fear I push play with my finger trembling.

"Hi Mav, it's Drea. Me and my girl are in H-town, just wanted to see if you were free. A few of us from training were planning to meet up at... hold up babe what's the name of that restaurant we going to?"

"For the 3rd time. Turkey Leg Hut," I hear a light feminine voice say.

"Yeah, Turkey Leg Hut. I heard their food is bangin! We're meeting there on Saturday at seven. I miss you, sis, Hit me back. And just in case you still want to say no, he's not coming. Hit me later."

The "him" I so desperately want to forget about is Lawrence Wilson a man that would be better left in the deep hiding spot I call my heart. He was the type of man who could tell you sweet lies that still sounded like the truth. Lawrence was more than just a stain from my past, he was a full-blown toxic spill and someone who I never intended on seeing ever again. The mention of him makes me feel like a crazed woman and even though years have passed since I last saw him my mind still remembers the hurt; he made me feel.

But the thought of seeing Drea makes me smile. It's been a long time since we've talked. She's one of the first female friends I ever felt close with. When we were first paired together as roommates, I felt we were complete opposites. She was a social butterfly while I was an outcast. If it wasn't for her, I don't know if I even would've made friends.

I think about saying no honestly, but then remember what I did last Saturday. An image of me on the couch with a bottle of wine, no glass, and re-runs of Girlfriends playing reminds me that I have not a damn thing planned.

I text Drea back: "Hey, getting ready for work. I got your message, and I'll be there. Love you, see you then."

She texts me back a purple emoji. "Bet"

I realize I can't make it on time to my workout since it's almost eight-thirty and I'll only have thirty minutes to get ready for work. I turn on my shower so it's hot enough to warm my skin and get ready for another tedious workday. I'm really meeting up with Drea after all this time, and I'm even more relieved knowing Lawrence won't be there. Smiling entirely too hard, I hop out of the shower naked and grab my Rose helping me to kick start my day.

Arriving at the office a few minutes past nine am I place my purse in my cabinet and scramble to the coffee machine. Ever since I moved to Houston and started working in the drone intelligence department, I've realized that being in the military has presented certain challenges. Since I've started this role there have only been two other black people in this department one being my Lieutenant. In a male-dominated industry, I've made it my business to never even look twice at any of the men in this building, so I don't damage my own reputation. As a result, I'm overlooked for new assignments because people think I'm intimidating, but the truth is I just want my work to speak for itself. I just need one big opportunity to make a name for myself.

For now, I've been given the assignment of reviewing drone feeds in France, one of the most elementary cases since the last time we had a conflict with them was in WWI. Although I think the feed is pointless there was some chatter about an unsanctioned regime placing threats on US diplomats.

Listening to countless conversations, some in English and French, I tap my temple ready for it to be five o'clock. I study my computer screen stopping for snacks every two hours until finally it's time to go and my weekend can officially start with a much-needed glass of pinot grigio waiting for me chilled in the fridge.

"Welcome to the Turkey Leg Hut. Will you be reserving a table?" the hostess asks.

"No, I believe my friend is already here, the last name would be McPherson."

"Yep, they're straight back and to the left, enjoy your meal."

Smiling nervously, I walk towards the back of the restaurant, my stomach doing somersaults with each step. My outward appearance shows the opposite of how I truly feel, I'm dressed in a yellow bodycon dress with my denim jacket and strappy thong sandals. Trying not to cause any attention to myself but feeling my ass jiggle with every step I reach the large table with enough seats for at least fifteen people. With her back to me, I can tell its Drea, with her signature cornrows and southern drawl.

"Hey stranger," I say tapping her on the shoulder.

"Bitch is this really you? You look good!"

Standing up from her chair we embrace in a hug that releases all my tension.

"I could say the same to you." We both marvel at each other for a second. And after the woman sitting next to Drea clears her throat very loudly Drea introduces me to her girlfriend.

"Yo my bad Mav, this is my girl, Kelis."

I throw on my best fake smile adding extra chipper to my voice even throwing in a compliment.

"Nice to meet you, Kelis I love your nails."

"Thank you," she says flatly and resumes staring into her phone.

"So what's going on in Houston, I heard you came out here after training and never looked back?"

"Something like that, I'm a senior analyst for the Surveillance department, but I really want a team of my own. In the last few years, I've trained two men who got promotions leading their own departments. I honestly feel stuck like there's no opportunity for me to grow. But I also love Houston."

"Yeah I feel you, I've been in Hawaii, Canada, and Guam all within the last two years. Shit we already knew it was hard being a woman in the military but it's becoming more challenging trying to move up."

"No lies told sis" Feeling like old times as if on cue our waiter brings a round for us three with a green liquid inside. Making eye contact with Drea I shake my head; I just know she's ordered some liquid marijuana our go-to when we were in training and would sneak out to Lucky Arcade Bar.

"For old time's sake," I smile, grabbing my shot and cheering with Drea and her girl. I smash the glass on the table ready for another round, allowing the liquid courage to settle my nerves.

"So , who all is coming to this reunion?"

"As you can see these motherfuckers still always show up late but it's Rich, Caleb you remember he was Lawrence's roommate?"

"Uhm yeah," just the brief mention of Lawrence's name makes my insides quiver fucking asshole I think silently.

"And I think Jackie and Terry."

"You mean crazy ass Jackie" laughing mostly to myself.

"No, she's not so crazy anymore, she left the Air Force about two years ago, now she's married with two kids."

"Wow, time really does fly... " shrinking into my seat.

Bitter thoughts leak in reminding me that I'm alone. Fighting that feeling of not being enough and having the perfect life I flag down our waiter requesting another round. After another ten minutes of catching up with Drea, I find out she and Kelis have been dating for three months and madly in love ever since.

The rest of our party walks in filling the large table. Feeling like the odd woman out since I don't have a date, I slide closer to Drea clinging to her like a lifeline. I share some brief conversations with Jackie and her husband who are sitting directly across from me.

Mostly though I tune out trying to make myself look intrigued by studying my phone screen. I scroll past the same pictures on Facebook I looked at an hour ago trying to make this awkward urge to go home pass. Just as I hear Lawrence's name being mentioned at the other end of the table another round of shots come. I've stopped counting how many I've had and simply raise my glass with everyone else.

"Cheers to this reunion, my girl, and this good ass food we're about to eat," Drea says.

"Cheers," we all say in unison.

Allowing the liquor to turn on my confidence and turn off my anxiety I strike up a conversation with Jackie about her life now as a mom. Paying close attention to how her husband smiles when she mentions the kids and hangs on to her every word.

Getting distracted, I stare at the ways his lips curl into a smile. I admire the way his full lips hide his teeth as he continues talking. I quickly turn my attention back to Jackie saying something about her new career as a real estate agent but get distracted by my overwhelming need to pee. Those liquid marijuana drinks ran straight through me.

Excusing myself from the table, I'm so tipsy I have to strain my eyes to find the bathroom. Finding the restroom in a darkly lit corner I rush to the small stall and grab my dress in one hand and the railing in the other. After freshening myself up I head back to our table slowly relishing the restaurant. A crowd of young black people enjoying the famous turkey leg and huge daiquiris draws my attention away from where I'm walking. I smash into the man walking in front of me.

"Shit, I'm sorry."

"It's all good, ma."

As soon as the word "ma" leaves his mouth I just know I'm having a panic attack mixed with the urge to slap this nigga square in his face.

"Lawrence?"

"Oh shit. What's good, ma? I haven't seen you in years."

A smile across his face shows all thirty-two teeth, but he's met with a grimace from me. Usually, his New York accent would make me melt but instead, all I want to do is look for an escape strategy to get away from him. I say nothing and saunter away in my bodycon dress, leaving him standing there.

Sitting next to Drea I give her a cold stare mouthing, "I thought you said he wasn't coming."

She shakes her head hastily just as Lawrence grabs a seat at the other end of the table.

*Yeah, that's right nigga. Stay far, far away from me,* I say under my breath. The energy at the table instantly shifts and it's so quiet we can hear Kelis' long ass nails typing on her phone.

"Leave it to Lawrence to fuck up a good night," Caleb says.

But instead of a serious facial expression both he and Lawrence bust into a fit of laughter. Somehow conversations resume and all tension dissipates. Except for me, I'm still fuming, dying to leave the restaurant.

The dinner moves on dreadfully slowly. I pick over my plate of jerk chicken tacos, losing my appetite with just a glance at the other end of the table. I don't know why I allowed him to have this power over me after all these years. He wasn't my first, but he was the first man I fell in love with. Even with all the lies I always believed he would change for me, for us but I was wrong.

Grabbing our waiter's attention I ask him for my bill and a to-go box, staring at my phone it's now nine-thirty. I can still watch reruns of my favorite show "Boys Over Flowers" if I leave now.

"All right everyone thank you all for coming out. It better not be another seven years before I see your asses again. The party hasn't stopped yet I got a table at Reign nightclub. I know some of y'all old asses are going home, but for the rest let's turn up!" Drea says enthusiastically.

After gathering all our food, I waive over the waiter again to request my check.

"Oh, sorry ma'am it appears that gentleman has already paid for your ticket," the waiter says pointing at Lawrence.

"Least he could fucking do," I mutter.

"I'm sorry. What was that?" the waiter asked me.

"Nothing, thank you." I pull a twenty dollar bill out of my pocket to give him a tip.

I grab my purse and decide to just ignore Lawrence for the rest of the night, but I need to talk to Drea before we head to the club. I deserve a night out; nothing is waiting for me at home except an empty apartment. After saying a brief goodbye to Jackie and her husband I see Drea by herself.

"Yo, Mav, before you get mad at me, I didn't know he was coming. He told me he would be out of town."

Rolling my eyes. I just stare blankly at her waiting for more words to come out of her mouth.

"Mav, really …. we haven't seen each other in years, don't let him fuck up your night. Come on, Grandma."

No longer able to maintain my anger I have to smile. "Grandma" was the nickname my drill Sergeant gave me in training on account of how slow I used to run before I got my body into good physical shape.

Finally giving in "Okay Drea, but just till eleven. I don't want to be out all night."

After a quick twenty-minute drive we arrive at Reign night-club, one of the most exclusive clubs in the city. The parking lot is littered with luxury cars from Bentleys to flashy Mercedes with large rims. It seemed like everyone in Houston was at Reign tonight. I step out of my car and stare up the long line to get into the club.

Staring down at my sandals I open my trunk ready to see what spare heels and accessories I have in case of emergencies like this one. I spot my black kitten heels I bought for my birthday and a wide belt I can accessorize with my dress. After applying some light makeup, I lay my jacket down on the passenger seat and walk towards the front of the club. Drea is standing beside security slowly waving me on.

"Mav, happy you made it I thought you might have chickened out and gone home, what took so long?"

"I just had to get myself together, I was dressed for dinner not the club," I say smiling.

"Ok let's get inside, I reserved a section for us. Heard this club gets packed on Fridays.

"Yeah, it's my first time here, but my sister says it's really nice."

Inside there are three tall stories of wide-open space to dance. Strobe lights, large velvet couches, and a wrap-around bar are in the center of the large room. The crowd is thick with patrons' women grinding on men with drinks in their hands as the latest hip-hop blares from the speakers above the dance floor. Feeling a little uncomfortable at the sight of all these people, I try not to bump into anyone. After a slew of "excuse Me's" we finally make it to a large oak table set up with bottles of liquor on ice and a few hookah pipes spread out on the large table.

I choose a safe spot on the velvet couch close enough to refill my cup but far enough to make a hasty exit. The music is blaring, and my head feels light from the drinks at the restaurant but the rest of my body pulses with excitement to finally being out of the house for the first time in months. My foot bounces to the music and my hips slowly move to my own personal rhythm, I let the music drown out everything else. Just as I refill my cup, I feel the intensity of a set of eyes on me. I know all too well it's Lawrence.

"Mind if I sit down?" Lawrence asks.

"It's a free country." Ridding myself of any desire for drama I scoot further away from him.

"I wanted to talk with you privately, I know this conversation is long overdue, but I want to say I'm sorry."

He gives me the saddest attempt to look like a sad puppy and waits for my response.

"Listen, Lawrence, what you did to me back then was fucked up. You embarrassed me and I could've gotten kicked out of the Force because of the actions you took. But we're both grown now so I won't hold any grudges, but you really should have just been honest with me. Besides, what happened to Valarie?"

"You know damn well her name was Valeria," he says.

"Yeah whatever, how's *Valeria* doing?"

We both laugh remembering the bowling alley incident and how I kept calling his then-girlfriend by the wrong name. But then I catch him, his eyes a little low probably from drinking. I see the same face that caused me so much pain, but I also remember the way he used to make me say his name. I told myself never again would I let him inside me, but his lusty eyes and this liquor have me ready to disobey.

"She passed away a few years ago in a car accident. Her family and I still talk occasionally."

A sad expression replaces the drunken one and instantly I feel like an asshole. He stares into his glass and gulps the brown liquor which I suspect is whiskey, his favorite.

"Shit, I'm sorry."

"It's okay, she broke up with me not too long after she came to visit and ended up marrying some guy from our neighborhood. But let's talk about you, what's your man like?"

"I don't have a man." *Now he knows damn well I don't have a man, if I did, he would be sitting next to me instead of Lawrence's fine ass.*

"Wow, all these years I'm really surprised you're not married with kids already. You were always such a good girl."

"Well, sometimes things don't work out the way you expect," I say somberly.

The air between us grows quiet again and I look around the club to distract myself from the heat building between my thighs. I notice some of the crowd has thinned out and more people are sitting down. Staring to my left I see Drea with her eyes trained on me and Lawrence. My eyes search hers trying to read her puzzled face.

"Maverick, do you ever think we could have worked out? If I'm being honest, you were always the one, I wondered about, the one that got away."

"I didn't get away; you threw me away when you lied to me and chose to be with another female." I slam my cup down on the table with my nostrils flaring in anger.

"You're right Maverick, but look can we just agree to leave the past behind us for tonight and only think about right now."

"Fine."

And I do just that, leaving the past where it should be. Me and Lawrence spend the rest of the night in our own personal world like we used to back in the day. He tells me about how his family is pressuring him to marry soon and start having children but as usual, he still wants to be a bachelor. I tell him how I haven't been on a decent date in years and how my apartment has the best view of Houston.

"So what are you doing after this?" I hear Lawrence say.

"Probably going home, I'm really tired, this is the latest I've been out in a long time" Finally letting my guard down I genuinely smile at Lawrence thinking about our conversation.

"So, what about showing me the best view of Houston?"

I peep at his not-too-subtle request to come back to my place. Normally I would say no immediately because of our history. But something deep in my body stirs and even though I know I shouldn't, the thought of not sleeping alone tonight guides my next sentence.

"I would love for you to see the view." In my most sultry tone I let my eyes indicate just how serious I am, batting my lashes and pouting my thick lips. I want him to see more than the city skyline and anticipate what's sure to be a good nightcap.

"Shit, well what are we waiting for, let's go now."

Lawrence hurriedly gets up, almost knocking the hookah stand over on the table."

"Slow down. I didn't say we were leaving together. Give me your number and I'll text you my address."

"Oh, so you don't want to be seen with me, huh?"

"I didn't say that but it's really no one else's business."

I leave Lawrence standing there and walk towards Drea and the rest of our group to say my goodbyes. I strategically avoid speaking to Lawrence again before I change my mind about what I'm about to do.

After exiting the club and switching back into my sandals I text Lawrence my address and drive quietly back to my apartment. I take a quick shower and change into a sexy bra and panties underneath my pink silk robe.

Staring up at the clock I realize it's after three in the morning. I light a candle and just as I turn on Mary J Blige's "Growing Pains" I hear a ding notification from my phone.

*Lawrence 3:15 am* **Are you still up?**

*Me 3:23 am* **Yes**

I type in my code to allow him to come upstairs. I wait patiently by the door getting mentally prepared for what my body needs tonight. Being a little too anxious I crack the door open before he even has time to knock and see he's still wearing the same attire from the club. I greet him with a smile and guide him into my apartment making sure I lead the way.

"So, this is the best view in Houston," I say.

The balcony doors are open and a quick crisp breeze sneaks in. Feeling my nipples get hard through my bra I'm reminded that tonight I need to take what my body has been craving.

"Yeah, that is a hell of a view."

Turning around, I see Lawrence's eyes moving up my body and his pupils trained at the opening of my robe where my breasts are pushed against the lace bra.

I walk to him with no more words needing to be exchanged. I grab the back of his neck and push our mouths together. His tongue assaults mine in a power play and I feel my mind start to get further away from my body. His smooth arms rub against mine trying to start some kind of fire. I'm lifted into the air in mere seconds, surprised by the change in gravity I hug Lawrence's neck tight with one swift move he slides my robe down, my ass is now on the marble kitchen counters.

As if on cue Mary J Blige's "Feel Like a Woman" starts playing and I just know this orgasm I'm about to have will be all worth it. Lawrence is kissing me like I'm about to disappear in front of his eyes leaving bite marks on my neck and nibbling on my ear. I can hardly stop myself when I reach for his belt buckle. But he stops me and aggressively pushes my torso down so my back is on the counter.

"Not yet, it's still my turn."

With a devilish grin on his face, he opens my legs wide and slowly plays with my womanly center. The lace thong panties stained with juices already he lowers his head and kisses my inner thigh. After blowing warm air onto my belly button, he finally proceeds to kiss me in that special place.

The only thing I hear in my normally quiet apartment is me gasping for air, my fingers digging into his scalp messing up the perfect waves on his head.

"Damn you taste good Mav, just like I knew you would."

I can't even fathom a sentence and just nod my head eyes shut tight, and mumble a quick "Mmm Hmm."

I feel a slight chill as he comes up for air, but I keep my eyes shut still reeling from the orgasmic body high he just gave me. Before I can even get a clear thought in my head I feel all of him inside of me. All my juices saturate his body, he pinches my nipples and just when I think it can't get any better he places his hands gently around my throat. With each pump inside of my body, he adjusts his grip and has me pinned to the counter. Ready to switch positions I try to push on Lawrence's chest but instead of his body shifting I hear a large growl escape his mouth. A few seconds later I feel his own juices sliding down my thigh.

I literally pinch myself thinking silently. *Did he really just come that quickly, and he came inside of me. What the actual fuck?*

"So how was that?" He looks belated thinking he's done some amazing job.

Not wanting to hurt his feelings I say, "Fantastic," giving him a fake smile.

"Yeah it was; forgot how tight you were, I just couldn't help myself."

"Yeah, okay. Well, see you later."

"See you later? Really Mav, you gon kick me out like that?"

"Yep, bye." I hop down from the counter and pick up my robe wanting to cover myself quickly.

I gather his things quickly in my hands and tap my foot anxiously waiting by the door. He continues to stare in disbelief; I guess that makes both of us.

"So you're dead ass serious, damn girl."

"Look I just don't want you to think anything is going to happen with us. You had your fun, it's time for you to go."

"Fine, be that way."

And with one final glare Lawrence takes his clothes and leaves. Giving myself a moment, I laugh out loud at the fact that Lawrence has become a two-minute man.

*Fuck. I could have just used my Rose toy.*

# Chapter 2

"Hi Sergeant Campbell, I was told you wanted to see me?"

"Sit down Lieutenant, now I called you in here to talk about your future in the Air Force."

"Am I in some kind of trouble?" concerned about what he could want to discuss.

"No, quite the opposite I've noticed your good eye for standing out as a leader, on top of that you don't take any shit. With an impeccable record like yours over the last seven years it's time you branch out."

"I appreciate that Sir, but I'm still unclear what this is all leading to. Can I frankly speak sir?" Sergeant Campbell nods his head permitting me to continue.

"It's been six months since I last applied for any position and every time I try to branch out as you put it I get overlooked. I can't train another man that just going to take the job I've worked hard to get."

"I'm going to cut to the chase. We have an opening in Seoul, South Korea and I put your name down as someone who can get the job done. We have a new team there, and we want the best the Air Force has to offer. I'm sure you've heard about recent nuclear threats coming out of North Korea. As such the Air Force is looking to increase its presence in Korea and gather new intel. The job starts in two weeks, more money, and you'd be taking the lead in our Air Surveillance Intelligence program. The job is yours if you want it.

*While my face is still one of calmness my insides jump. This type of opportunity is once in a lifetime. I think about the weight of a chance, my chance. But what about my life here? Could I just pick up and leave that easily? Of course you can,* my inner voice says.

"Wow, I wasn't expecting this. Thank you, sir. Do I have time to think about it before making my decision?"

"You've got till the end of the week; after that they will look for someone else to fill the role" he says.

I scramble to get out of the chair, shocked I'm finally getting the recognition I deserve. Just as I make my way towards the door dismissing myself, I turn around once more.

"Robinson, a chance like this only comes once in a lifetime. Especially for black officers like you and me. Just think about it."

"Okay, I will. Thank you again, Sergeant Campbell."

After taking the rest of the afternoon to weigh my decisions my stomach seems to have constant butterflies. I drive home with only one thing on my mind. A once-in-a-lifetime opportunity like this could change my career forever, but what about my life here in Houston?

My doorbell rings, breaking my concentration and checking my camera. I see it's just the Chinese food I ordered. Quickly opening the door, I pick my food up from the welcome mat and place it on the counter. As soon as I sit back down on the couch, I hear a chime on my phone.

NOTIFICATION: Flo Period App // Your period is late by 6 weeks and (1) day.

*What?* I try to remember the last time my period came on and draw a mental blank. Pacing over to the calendar I keep on the refrigerator I notice my period tracker app is right. I'm late.

"It can't be." The words left my lips before I could catch them.

Growing more frantic by the minute I run to my bathroom and open the second drawer reaching for the only item that can confirm my suspicion. I run back to the fridge for some bottled water and after ten minutes I'm able to pee on the stick that will determine my fate.

After pacing a hole into my floor for five minutes the pregnancy test finally shows my results. There are two solid lines, I'm pregnant. A wave of anxiety hits me like a brick wall. Deciding to take this new job just got way more complicated. Lawrence is the only man I've slept with. He is not the man I want to have a baby with. He's immature and doesn't want to have a family with me or any other woman for that matter. *Why now?*

Staring at the Houston skyline I try to think about me being someone's mom. The dream of coming home to my husband and child is shattered. All I can seem to picture is me standing alone holding a child's hand with no one there to help me. No one there to lift my belly, go with me to doctors' appointments, no one to share my life with. Being a single mom was never in the cards for me. Not before and definitely not now.

My eyes tear up for what I know is about to come. The selfish part of me wins this internal battle and I reach back into my second drawer. While my hands shake to open the Plan B box, I try to block out any feelings of guilt.

"I'm not ready."

Swallowing the last of my water, I gulp down the pill and any regrets about my decision.

***

It's been a few days since I officially confirmed taking the position in Seoul. My excitement seems to be replaced by worry as I stare beside me admiring my sister Shaunie relaxing in the spa chair. Her feet are planted in the soak tub, as a nail tech walks by and hands us both a glass of champagne. Our weekly nail pedicure appointments that we've had ever since she moved to Houston two years ago.

Her short jet-black pixie cut, thick eyelashes, and caramel skin remind me of my mother. She's only 5"2" but you couldn't tell she has the energy of a five-year-old in the body of a grown woman. My family always said she got her looks from mom while I got mine from my dad.

Shaunie looks up from her phone and shows me a picture of a space she's thinking of leasing for her new hair salon.

"I'm telling you I'm not working for any more of these dumb ass salons ever again. I'm getting my own spot" she says venting to me about how her current salon is always filled with drama.

"Well speaking of jobs I got a new offer" I tap my nails lightly on the small table top waiting to say more.

"Look at my girl doing the damn thing, where is the Air Force sending my girl now?" My sister Shaunie asks.

"Seoul" letting the words hang in the air like helium in a balloon. I pause waiting for Shaunie's reaction.

"Oh girl what part of the US will that be in?"

"Shawnie Seoul, South Korea… like in a whole other hemisphere. Who's gone do my hair over there, or do me for that matter? You know there's barely any black people there."

"Girl, it's black people everywhere and if there aren't any in Seoul, just send big sis a ticket and I'm there. Can't help you with the man thing but I'm sure there are some good-looking ones just waiting to get their own piece of chocolate."

"You're a mess," I say laughing at her statement. "On the one hand I've been waiting for a break like this in my career for a few years. I would have the opportunity to lead my own team. But then I think of leaving my life behind here, with my family. I just don't know what to do. I'm almost 30 with no kids, I've only been in one serious relationship my whole life. How am I going to change all that in a different country? It feels like I have to choose which is more important."

"Okay, number one, bitch, you are 26, not 30 don't push it. And secondly that stuff doesn't matter. You could meet the man of your dreams anywhere. There's still time. As for family, girl forget about us. The last time I checked they have phones, airplanes, and internet in other countries."

"But what if I can't connect with anyone there, Shaunie? You know it takes a long time for me to trust people, let alone build a relationship. What if I can't handle this?"

"And what exactly have you done here in Houston, sis? You've been here for over five years. I never saw you mention a date with another dude since that Lawrence guy. And that shit you do on Tinder doesn't count. Just fucking a guy and ghosting him isn't a real attempt at a relationship. I know you're afraid but really what are you leaving behind here?"

"I haven't done that in over two years," I say quietly not addressing any other points she made.

"Exactly my damn point. Look little sis, you have to make the best decision for yourself. There's nothing holding you, no kids or man. Family will be here when you get back. Besides, you have always wanted to run your own operation and travel the world. I really don't see a dilemma; you just have to trust yourself."

"Damn, I hate when you get like this, sounding right and shit. How are you so sure everything is going to work out?"

"Because I know you, Mav. Aren't you the same woman who scored the highest score out of your class on the ASVAB?"

"Yes."

"And who aced their exam the first time to become a drone operator?"

"Okay, I get your point but you also forgot bad bitch."

"Yeah okay, whatever. But really sis you got this, just trust in yourself for once. Let the real you take flight, okay?"

Sealing the deal, I nod my head okay and swing my pinky in the air waiting for Shaunie to do the same. We link pinky's, a childhood action to confirm my promise to her.

Leaning back in the spa chair I press the remote and turn on the massage feature feeling hopeful.

# Chapter 3

"My flight leaves at 6am, Shaunie!" I shout through my apartment applying some light eyeshadow to my lids.

"Oh, come on it's your last night in Houston. The least you can do is get drunk with your big sis. I mean for the next four years when will we have the chance to do this again?"

"Wow! You really know how to guilt trip me, Shaunie. Okay, but we need to get back at least before 1 am. You're lucky I only need to pick out my outfit for tomorrow."

I walk to the living room and debate if I want to go out but it's too late.

"Great, it's settled, we're about to get lit!" Shaunie says.

Taking a longing glance out the balcony doors of my high-rise condo I think of how much I'll miss this view. A long sip of my Stella Rosa wine makes me think back to the first day I moved into my condo.

It was like yesterday when Shaunie and her then-boyfriend Eric helped me move all my furniture and clothes in. The brown leather sectional required all three of us, mostly Eric, to maneuver through the doorway. I remember feeling so alone in the apartment because I had grown so used to sharing living spaces. But over the years the high-rise apartment in uptown Houston had become my place of refuge, a safe haven.

Houston holds a lot of memories for me. I started my career after training in the Air Force and was able to grow my career over the last five years. It was a new start for me after getting my heart broken into pieces. All I wanted to do was get rid of any previous existence of my previous life and start something new.

Even though I was at the top of my class academically, I always struggled socially with others, especially women. While being at the top of my rank was a blessing to my career it was a curse to my social life. Most of my female bunkmates thought I was a goody-two-shoes, most of the men did, too. Once I got my heart broken and showed my ass, I could count on my hand how many "friends" I truly had.

My first adult love, Lawrence, was an army brat and enrolled against his father's wishes in the Air Force because he always wanted to be a pilot. He came from old money and barely passed his ASVAB but because of his family name and clout, he made it. He was reckless and I was safe; classic opposites attract.

When I first met him, his smart mouth and arrogance turned me off but once I got to know the man behind these actions, I fell for him, hard. It was a bonus that he was handsome and had the body of a brown god. His face was a cross between Michael B. Jordan and Damson Idris. Every girl wanted him and plenty of them did. Lawrence, to put it lightly, was a hoe and soon I found out why girls were going crazy for him.

One time he had to hide out in my bunk for eight hours because he had had sex with a girl that started stalking him at chow, combat, and shower time. He couldn't escape her. It was the first time he secretly spent the night with me.

My roommate Aundrea was cool with Lawrence on account of her being a lesbian. She never looked twice at him and had just as much pull as he did with the ladies. They became friends instantly ranking all the girls in training and sharing laughs about our commanding officer. Aundrea was out on a date enjoying her civilian time when I heard a special knock at the door just as I was about to put on my headphones and re-read some letters from my family.

Knock three times, pause and then knock four more times. It was a special knock that let me know somebody needed help. A special code me and Aundrea created for our group when they needed us. Hopping off the bed quickly I opened the door without checking through my peephole. In the hall in sweats and a NY Yankees hat was Lawrence.

"Hey Mav, is Aundrea here?"

"Nope, she's on a date. You used the secret knock. Do you need to come in, or were you just messing around?"

"Nah this is urgent. I need a place to hide out for a while; you know that chick Jackie."

"Yeah, she's from squad 4, what about her?"

"She's fucking loony, I was in my bunk with Caleb and she pops up out of nowhere with a cake at our door."

"I don't see anything wrong with that, like damn is it your birthday or something and you didn't tell anyone?"

"Hell no, apparently the cake is for our one-week anniversary."

Looking at Lawrence's face to gauge his seriousness I bust out laughing once I know he's dead-ass serious. Almost in tears from laughing so hard, I say, " So when you hit your two-week anniversary you giving Jackie a ring, right?"

"Get the fuck outta here."

I laugh even harder as his New York accent comes out, but he just continues on.

"Ma is acting mad dumb. I told her from the beginning it was only sex no relationship. Fuck I look like wife-ing a girl at 19. On top of that, she let me hit the first night. How many other dudes she let hit? My future wife gotta be all innocent and shit like you."

"Oh really? In your dreams. Besides you have a lot of options already on top of that I'm not interested."

"That's what they all say until I get inside here," he points to my head, "and there," pointing towards my feminine middle.

I shake my head mockingly and just for a second our eyes meet and the room gets quiet. Not wanting to give him the upper hand I glance down at my letters while sitting on the bed and pretend to re-read my mom's letter to me. She sent it my first week of training explaining how Dad is finally getting his man cave after they finally finished renovating our basement back in Charleston, SC. She went on to explain the room is covered in Clemson gear and how he never comes upstairs anymore.

Tired of pretending to read my letter, I glance up and see Lawrence on Aundrea's bed, his eyes meeting mine again for the second time tonight. The oddest sensation sweeps over me, my brown cheeks flushing and stomach full of butterflies. It's like he knew I was staring at him, before things get any more awkward, I hear the lock click and see Aundrea sauntering in with a wide smile.

"Hey roomie," she waves at me. "Hey asshole," she gives Lawrence the finger. "What the hell are you doing on my bed?"

"I obviously couldn't stay in mine. Jackie is acting way out of line. She baked me a cake talking about our anniversary, and she's been stalking me all week. I gave her the d*** and now she can't handle it."

"Damn, so you mean to tell me 5'2, 140 pounds-soaking-wet Jackie got my man hiding out?" Similar to my reaction Aundrea can't contain her laughter.

"Was it worth it?" Drea has the most mischievous look on her face.

Catching onto what she means I instantly tune out not ready to hear this part of the conversation. I quickly locate my headphones on the nightstand and grab my iPod ready to blast Tha Carter II. Slowly closing my eyes I let my dreams take me somewhere far away.

***

"So am I going to have to drink this shot on my own or are you joining me?"

I turn around so lost in the past, Shaunie has my bottle of White Hennessey on the granite island with two shot glasses lined up. Mentally preparing myself for one last night of fun. I walk in through my sliding glass doors and prop myself on the island feeling its cool surface up against the Texas heat, I take one last look at the city skyline.

"Of course not," reaching for my shot glass I say " A toast to new beginnings and sharing my last night in Houston with the best person in the world!"

"Cheers!" Shaunie gulped down the shot hungrily, feeling a little impulsive.

I reach for the bottle and down the second shot just as quickly. I feel the hot sting in my chest reminding me that I'm not a heavy drinker but just as soon as the feeling comes it goes.

Suddenly needing to hype myself up I look for my remote in search of music. After selecting YouTube, I choose the perfect song to start our night. "Cash S***" by Megan Thee Stallion and Da Baby. It's something about when these two pair up together I just love, instantly I start doing my little two-step and shake my ass a little, but I look over and Shaunie is full-fledged twerking.

"See sis, this is how you do it." She then proceeds to slap her ass and clap her cheeks. And with that visual, I decide it's time to go to my room and get dressed. Searching through my bare closet since most of my clothes are packed, I try to look for something I can wear for a night out.

Finally, after searching for a few minutes I settle on my hip-hugging Seven jeans, a royal blue cross-back halter top, and my gold Alexander Wang heeled sandals. Looking for one last item to complete my look I see the gold diamond hoops that Lawrence bought me for my birthday, of all the shit I threw out from him I just couldn't bear to get rid of them.

I tread back into the kitchen for another shot watching Shaunie twerk to some City Girls song that I don't know. I shouldn't be surprised she even has all this energy.

After feeling the sting in my throat and chest once more from another shot I start getting dressed. Styling my knotless braids into a high bun after applying some lip-gloss to complete my look I'm ready to go.

# Chapter 4

Later that night after we get home, I text Shaunie:

*ME 1:20am: Thanks sis, I had a good time*

*SHAUNIE 1:21am: I'm going to bed*

*ME 1:23am: Love you*

Within a few minutes my head hits the pillow, and my dreams take over.

"Hey ma," Lawrence.

"Hey yourself," I say smiling at his pet name for me.

Standing in the middle of his doorway I look at him. Admiring the way his Levi's hang low at his hips and his white, collared Ralph Lauren shirt looks so out of place on his body. He normally wears sweats or a uniform.

"I thought you were going to get that thing handled today. What are you doing up and walking around?" he asks, hinting at the fact that I should be resting. He acts like taking a Plan B means I have to be on bed rest.

"I did; I just wanted to see you before I went to lay down. I know you're expecting your sister to visit today, but I just wanted to check on you."

"I'm straight ma, just worry about yourself."

Immediately hearing the tone of his voice makes me shudder. It's so cold, like we haven't spent the last four months learning how to love each other. Our secret love affair feels like a mistake with just a sentence.

"Oh really? Lawrence, that's how you feel?" I scrunch up my face prepared to head straight to my room.

" I'm sorry I didn't mean it like that Mav, I just have a lot on my mind today. I am worried about you."

"Well, I think there are better ways for you to tell me that, especially after what I just did to keep our little secret."

"You're right ma, I'm wrong as usual. I'm going to get ready for my sister to arrive. Then maybe I'll stop by later and make you feel all better."

In an instant, he pulls me into the room with the door closed. My heartbeat quickens just like anytime I'm around him and even with the abortion weighing on my mind he finds a way to make all thoughts cease. I'm so distracted by the sensation of his whispering in my ear I don't even know what the hell he's saying. I just nod my head and give him a quick peck on the cheek.

"I'll see you later," I say, escaping his trance and bedroom eyes.

Slowly twisting the doorknob and heading back towards my room, avoiding any glances that come my way, I meekly enter my room and land softly on my bed. At peace with the silence in the room I reach for my journal and start to write.

All the things I want to say out loud but can't start spilling onto the white pages. I think about how as a woman in the military I can't legally get an abortion, and had to purchase my Plan B pill in secret making sure to discard the box in the Walgreens bathroom.

I don't feel bad about my decision because I am not ready to be someone's parent, and neither is Lawrence. He was so sure the "pull out" method would work, and just like a dummy I believed him. I start scribbling faster, thinking if anybody from my family knew they would kill me. That is except my mom. She would be proud that me, her daughter, made the choice for herself. With all these things on my mind floating around I know this is a secret I'll die with, never telling a soul.

Just as I put my pen down a wave of nausea comes over me and I rush to my trash can. I throw up the blueberry muffin I had this morning feeling the sting of citrus in my throat from the orange juice. Another wave of side effects hits my body as I feel strong cramps in my abdomen. I quickly crawl back into bed ready to spend this Saturday locked in my room. Focusing on the popcorn ceiling above I think of life a few years from now, a life in which I'm ready to be someone's mother.

I hear a slight closing of the door and hear Drea's voice as she enters.

"Girl you've been missing all day, wake up!" She slaps my blanket playfully.

"Yeah I know. Just trying to catch these extra z's before Monday. You know we have that new physical to complete."

"Shit! I forgot about that, well anyway everyone's going bowling to that spot on Hunter Lane. You want to come?"

"Who all is going?"

With only one person in mind I try to play off how eager I must look. The chance to meet Lawrence's sister would be cool considering she's in town.

"Everybody in our normal crew, and Lawrence said something about his girl coming, too."

Not wanting to get alarmed or put my business out for Drea to know I try to hide my nervousness.

"Oh, you mean his sister that flew in from New York?" I try to correct her, knowing there's been a mistake.

"No his girlfriend. It's crazy to think this dude has been smashing all these chicks while he's here but has a whole girlfriend. I can't wait to see how his ass plays this off."

Remaining cool on the outside but burning on the inside, I try to keep my face as neutral and uninterested as possible.

"You know what? I'm going to take a few aspirins and go with you guys. What time are we leaving?"

"In 30 minutes," Drea said.

"Good. Just enough time for me to get ready."

I quickly grab my toiletry items and a towel. Walking as quickly as I can to the showers, I make it to the first shower stall before the first tear starts sliding down my face. I replay my conversation with Drea in my mind.

Even though no one's in the bathroom with me I try to mask my cries with the sound of the water. Streams of water and my tears mixing. Trying to focus on cleaning my body all I envision is Lawrence with another girl. Kissing her, fucking her, whispering sweet promises in her ear. *Does she even know about me?*

He played me like a fiddle, trying to keep our relationship a secret to "protect us." *Bastard.* I punch the tile in front of me so hard my knuckles bleed a little from the pain. I don't care, that's how much my heart hurts right now. The only thing motivating me right now to go out is revenge.

I scrub my body vigorously trying to wipe away any hurt. Allowing the hot water to cascade down my body I think of the perfect plan to get even, even though I know it will be petty, but I give zero fucks.

After I finally find the strength to finish my shower, I walk back to my room with a new found sense of pleasure to replace my pain. Preparing for a fight I tuck my hair in a tight ponytail, put Vaseline on my face, and throw on some sweats and my black Nikes. I put the finishing touch on my face, black mascara, to hide my puffy red eyes from crying.

"Damn, Mav. I said we going bowling, not to the gym."

"I'm comfortable in this besides I won't need to be dressed up for what we're doing," venom dripping from my voice.

"True, we are just bowling. Okay, well let's head out the door, the Uber is outside to take us. I think everybody else has already left."

"Okay, I'm ready." With one last look in the mirror I walk behind Drea ready to get even whatever the cost.

We walk into the AMF bowling alley with the stench of stale feet and glowing, shiny neon lights. It's like we've taken a step back into the nineties with the hardwood bowling lanes and old monitors used to keep score. There's a large bay window where I spot Caleb first and off to his right Lawrence's back is turned, standing between the legs of who I assume to be his girlfriend. Instantly feeling my cheeks flush, me and Drea walk to the check in counter.

"Can I have a size 10?" Drea asked.

"Sure, and for you, ma'am?" the pimply faced teen clerk asks.

"I'm good, I don't need them."

"Really Mav, you bowling in your sneakers?" Drea asks me.

I shoot her a look that instantly silences her and she grabs her shoes with me trailing behind her towards our group of friends.

"Hey! Y'all ready to get your asses handed to you? I'm scoring no less than a 290." Drea challenges, while motioning rolling an invisible bowling ball and smiling.

After a few moments, Lawrence finally turns around towards the group. His eyes bug out when he notices me standing beside Drea but he quickly recovers and switches his line of sight quickly. He doesn't even acknowledge me and quickly grabs the hands of the girl sitting down.

"Later for that shit, but before we get started, I want everybody to meet my girl Valeria, before any of you niggas try to fuck with her, don't."

Everyone laughs except me and Valeria, who doesn't seem amused.

"Yo, LJ don't do that shit, papi,. Don't act like since we in front of all these people I won't mush your ass."

"Ma, come on I'm just joking," he winks at her with the same look he gives me and wraps his arms around her tiny waist.

Putting my plan into action I walk around our group of friends to get closer to Valeria. I look her up from head to toe before stepping any closer as Lawrence turns his head to talk to Caleb. She's beautiful with her sandy blonde hair, big brown eyes, and long manicured nails. She kind of reminds me of Zoe Saldana, but she has a bigger chest; her mesh black jumpsuit leaves nothing to the imagination. Second guessing my own outfit, I look down at my baggy sweatpants but remember what I'm here to do.

"Hi, I'm Maverick," I say, extending my hand to her. But instead of being met with a handshake I am greeted with two empty faces. Valeria just stares down at my hand like a foreign object, while Lawrence's eye twitches standing behind her.

" Yo, what's up," she shrugs.

Already annoyed, I try to continue the awkward conversation.

"Lawrence didn't introduce me but I'm his girl, I mean friend girl," acting innocent of my stumbling of words I continue. "So Valarie, how long have you and Lawrence been together?"

"Valeria," she says slowly enunciating every letter.

"My bad, I mean Valeria."

Obviously annoyed, Valeria pushes her breath dramatically before saying, "We grew up together." Simple and offering no further explanation before turning her attention back to our group of friends.

Our lane is finally open and everyone spills into the seats ready to start the game. Caleb orders a round of drinks for everyone as we all settle into the plastic chairs.

Thinking about what I'm about to do, I have no remorse for this girl. She has a slick mouth and even though Lawrence is the reason she's about to get this ass whoopin I won't mind teaching her some manners.

Pretending I'm on an invisible chess board, I make the move that I know will set shit off. I make sure my hair is tucked away and patiently wait for Lawrence to take his turn to bowl.

A round of drinks arrive. I strategically ordered the frozen strawberry margarita just for this moment.

Walking up to Valeria one final time I pour the liquid over her sandy blonde hair with no explanation and completely catch her off guard. There's frozen alcoholic slush on her hair, her jumpsuit, and the floor. Lawrence quickly turns around giving me a deathly stare.

"What the hell, Mav?"

"Just wanted to give your sister the proper welcoming."

"Bitch!" she screams, lunging at me but missing as Lawrence grabs her from behind. She's so pissed speaking in Spanish now.

"Mav, you fucked up! I should let Valeria beat your ass for this shit. What's this even about?"

"Oh, like you don't know. How about the fact that we've been fucking for the last few months, or how you said your sister was coming to visit you, not your girl. You've been lying to me the whole fucking time." I conveniently don't mention the abortion.

"You mental. Everybody knows the only reason why you're even allowed to hang around us is Drea," he says pointing her way. "On top of that, Valeria is the only mami I'm checking for." Further embarrassing me he turns to Valeria.

"Babe, don't listen to this hoe, she's just jealous and wants some attention. I knew she had a crush on me but I ain't know the bitch was a stalker. I've been faithful to only you, baby."

I know I look stupid and crazy, but my jaw is on the floor from this bold-faced lie he's telling. Waiting for someone, anyone to jump to my defense, I'm stunned that no one is saying anything. The "friends" I thought I had seem to be looking on in surprise. Even Drea has nothing to say, even though they all know Lawrence has been fucking multiple girls. The chill of loneliness stings with no one on my side.

"I'm about to beat your ass! No one fucking does that to me. *Perra Negra.*" Valeria screams.

Instead of Lawrence holding her back this time his arms are by his side and Valeria lunges towards me again. She connects her fist with my jaw and tackles me to the wooden floor creating an even larger scene. Not allowing her to continue pummeling my face, I knee her in the stomach and start placing blows all over her body. Just as I really start to get into things, I feel a strong set of arms wrap around me. Caleb's long arms trap me in a bear hug while Valeria is dragged off in the opposite direction by Lawrence.

"Get off of me!" I scream as Caleb finally lets go.

"Yo Mav, tell me that shit isn't true! You've been fucking him. I told you he was a dog to females," Drea said close to my ear.

"Don't ask me shit! Now all of a sudden you want to talk. No one said anything when this nigga stood there lying. Everybody knows he has been messing around with multiple girls since we got here. Yet no one came to my defense when he was talking shit."

"But.." Drea tried to speak.

"Save it, I'm out of here. And don't say shit to anybody, especially to Sergeant Ramirez. Don't forget I got dirt on all of y'all!" I wave an accusing finger at the group of people I thought were my friends.

With a final glance towards the other end of the bowling alley Lawrence and Valeria are tongue-tied causing my heart to ache even more.

As all the adrenaline leaves my body from the fight, heavy nausea replaces it. Reminding me that the Plan B must still be affecting my body. After a few minutes my Uber finally shows up and I can cry in silence. The driver keeps quiet with a concerned look and low jazz on the radio. My heart breaks with each mile I get closer to base and further away from him.

# Chapter 5

It's been a little over twenty-four hours since I left Houston. My hair looks a mess, and a Nike track suit hangs off my body loosely as I stand with shaky legs from my seat waiting to be let off the plane. I'm tempted to kiss the ground as I exit the ramp and head to get my luggage.

Following behind the other passengers, I walk into a grand room with different departure gates. I see my first glimpse of the city; a large window overlooking the runway strip immediately to my left stops me in my tracks. My eyes sparkle with wonder as I continue looking back and forth between my new home and the people watching.

After a few more minutes of observing I realize it's time to go. Walking to a large escalator going down, I head in search of my luggage and look to my phone for instructions on what's next.

Stepping off the escalator I see a young Asian woman holding up a sign with my name on it. I slowly approach her hesitant since I'm not sure if she speaks English and quite honestly surprised.

I slowly say, "Hi, I'm Maverick Robinson, the new intelligence officer."

"Hi, Lieutenant Robinson, nice to meet you. I am Jin Choy. I'll be helping you get around and escorting you to your new housing. How was your flight?"

"Long. Texas is pretty far from here. I was so nervous about trying to find my way around Seoul. I haven't even claimed my bags yet, thought I would get lost for sure."

"That's no problem, I'd be happy to help. Let's get your bags."

As if on cue, we head towards a series of signs all in Korean but a big yellow sign with a luggage picture points straight ahead. Allowing Jin to take the lead I feel a world away from having any sense of direction.

Once we get to my assigned carousel, I see the aqua and purple luggage set I purchased gliding to me. I pick up my bags and walk with Jin out to the pick-up area where a government-issued GMC Yukon SUV is waiting. The driver's side door opens instantly with another agent emerging from the driver's seat.

Surprisingly he has the same dark skin as me, giving me a sense of hope that there are more black people in South Korea. No words are exchanged as my luggage is placed in the trunk, then me and Agent Choy get in the backseat of the car.

The dark-skinned man that helped with my bags shifts the car into drive, taking off into the traffic surrounding the terminal.

"Lieutenant Robinson, I'm Dak, your new driver. Welcome to Seoul." Pleasantly surprised, I hear an accent suggesting Dak is British.

"Nice to meet you, Dak. I have my own personal driver, that's great to hear. So, we'll spend a lot of time together."

"You could say that" he says, winking through the rearview mirror.

The air grows awkwardly silent giving me time to focus on my new surroundings. Never in my life would I think a simple girl like me would be moving across the globe starting a whole new life again. Staring out the window I admire all the large buildings and busy streets filled with people, making it feel a little like home.

We pass by some kind of street market with Korean signs and food stalls. Allowing curiosity to get the best of me I roll down the window and smell the air, it smells unfamiliar.

"Lieutenant Robinson," Jin spoke but I wasn't paying attention.

"Huh? Oh yes, please call me Mav, I didn't hear what you said."

"Just that we will be arriving at the new office first before Dak takes you to your new apartment. We would like to introduce you to the new team you'll be leading. They are anxious to meet you."

"Great I'm excited to get to work." Retreating into the seat I continue observing my new surroundings enjoying the ride.

After driving for another fifteen minutes, we arrive at a large concrete building with an American flag and South Korea flag planted in the center of a patch of grass. Examining the outside, it seems oddly displaced among all the historic looking buildings in Seoul.

"Lieutenant Robin—I mean Maverick, we're here. Please leave your luggage in the car. Dak will be here when it's time to leave," Jin instructed.

"Dak can speak for his damn self. Listen, once you're all finished just send me a text." Although his tone points towards all seriousness his face shows a hint of a smile.

I comply, unlocking my phone and handing it to him. A few finger touches to the screen and Dak saves his number in my phone.

"Okay, I think we're ready," Jin says firmly, getting out of the truck first.

Feeling like this for the second time today, I feel so lost but also anxious for what's to come. I follow Jin through the double doors and to a large round security desk.

"Hello Allen, this is the new Lieutenant Maverick Robinson," Jin announced.

"Good morning, nice to meet you," I say.

"Pleasure's all mine," Allen responded.

He swiftly hands me a security identification envelope including my badge, a new phone, and a stack of documents.

"If you'll follow me to the elevators, I'll introduce you to the team now," Jin tells me.

"Okay, Jin. Thanks Allen," I wave gleefully and walk down the long marble hallway. All I can hear are my heels clicking and the hum of the air conditioning system.

The ride up to the eighth floor is quiet. Stepping off the elevator, I'm led to a large conference room with agents sprinkled throughout the large area. The buzz of conversation stops as we enter the room. Not expecting too much diversity I see the room split with the

Korean agents centered around the left side of the room and American agents in the far-right corner.

"Good morning, everyone, your attention, please. We have our new head of drone surveillance here, Lieutenant Maverick Robinson."

Although no introduction is made, I know this is Colonel Davis, as we've been corresponding back and forth about my arrival. He has a military buzz cut and no-nonsense voice that could make a grown man second guess speaking to him. Even with just using his normal authoritative voice his white skin has a hint of red and the vein near his left eye seems to pulsate with each word.

"Hi, everyone, as mentioned I will be taking over reviewing our drone intelligence. I'm excited to get to work and connect with our counterintelligence as a team for both the American and South Korean benefit."

As the last word falls from my lips, I try to fake my confidence with a final smile and try to look as many people in the eye as I can. The room remains quiet with only the dry office air hanging in the moment. Colonel Davis resumes his introduction of me, mentioning my previous experience in Houston; mostly briefing the department about their plans to enroll North Korean diplomats to get intel.

Once the meeting is finished, I shake a slew of hands to which I can't remember anyone's names. The room is almost clear when a tall Asian man walks in starting to converse with the other Korean agents. He has an air of confidence that makes me take a second look at his appearance. A navy blue peacoat, and black slacks lay on his tall frame, while black leather loafers are on his large feet. My eyes finally reach his face: dark piercing eyes, surprisingly full lips, and a mid-length bowl cut. Normally I only find black men attractive but it's something unique about the way his six-foot frame looks and the slight tan that adorns his skin.

I notice us both staring at one another, but this mystery man makes no attempt to introduce himself. Even though we're working as a team I feel the division between the American and Korean agents.

This place seems to lack any sense of comradery, something I hope to change once I officially start managing the department.

Agent Jin appears out of nowhere and ushers me out of the large boardroom. I catch the mystery man still staring at me and remind myself to look him up once I have access to my work laptop.

"I hope you enjoyed meeting the team for now. I figure you are pretty tired so Dak will drive you to your new place here in the city. He's waiting downstairs for you."

"Understood, thank you Jin."

After navigating back to the elevator, I send a quick text to Dak that I'll be heading downstairs. I walk back to the truck and see he is already standing outside to open my door.

Once he gets back into the driver's seat, he turns on some music and a familiar song comes on by Prince.

"Wow, so you listen to Prince. I'm really surprised."

"What? Black British men can't listen to Prince?"

"No I mean–"

"I'm just fucking with you, but yeah Prince is one of my favorites."

"Mine too."

The conversation between us is more like old friends than new ones as we talk about music the whole ride over to my new apartment in a neighborhood off Hanok Street.

As the truck finally pulls up to a large building with balconies and plants all over the landscape, I start to think my new home won't be so bad.

"I was wrong about you. I thought you would be one of those stuck-up Americans but you're actually pretty cool."

"You are too," I respond, just as I grab the door handle to exit the truck. Dak looks at me through the rearview mirror.

"You take care of yourself."

"I will," giving him one final glance I grab my bags and head into the new place I will call home.

# Chapter 6

Unlocking the door to apartment 5C I get my first glance at international living. The apartment is cozy; with one look at the large windows I can see the interior of the apartment. An area to place my shoes is right next to the door across from a large mirror.

I open the next random door I see in the hallway. A light flickers on and I notice the bathroom. It's about half the size of my bathroom back in Texas but it still looks clean and bright. I manually turn the light off and keep exploring my new surroundings. Next, I see the kitchen, a small washing machine is under the sink and three cabinets line the small kitchen. *I wonder where the dryer is. Or was that the dishwasher?*

Drawn back to the window I can see the landscape of Seoul in the afternoon. Even though the city has some traditional looking buildings not far from the apartment it appears the city is quite lively. People roaming the streets, carts selling food, and a buzz of excitement permeates the air.

After people-staring a few moments longer I walk up a narrow set of stairs to my studio bedroom. My bed is on the floor, bare, and a large lamp provides the only light in the room. A dark wooden wardrobe is against the far side of the room, big enough for my belongings to fit inside. I can look down and see the entire living room from this view. I'm so exhausted between traveling and meeting my new team, but I'm hungry and really need a few things from the store to get settled in.

Gathering my purse, a small jacket, and my shoes I am ready to conquer this new place. After walking for about five minutes, I stumble into a store called Home Plus.

Navigating around the large department store I grab a cart and start throwing in bed sheets, pillows, shower curtains, anything that will help fill my new home. Slowly rounding the corner, I run into the last person I ever expected to see. The tall mysterious man from earlier I saw in the conference room, he's standing in front of a large row of bean bag chairs. I start to slowly walk past him wanting to go unnoticed but just as I pass the display he starts talking.

"Hi, is your name Maverick?"

"Yes, that's me. I saw you earlier at my briefing, and your name is?"

Extending my hand, he looks at it blankly. Remembering the customs in this culture I quickly extend my left hand. His skin touches mine just for a second, but electricity passes between us.

"Jun Pyo."

He says nothing more and again his eyes seem to be holding mine in his vision. His face a hue of red and my cheeks glowing with heat I start talking about something that will put out the fire inside.

"Okay, well what do you do in the Intelligence department?"

"I review most of the intel from North Korea. So, we'll be working very closely together."

"Wow. Then I look forward to working with you."

"I see you're getting settled in," he says, taking a long stare at my full basket now overflowing with multiple houseware items. Looking at the cart I suddenly remember I have no car here.

"Yeah, it seems I underestimated how much I can carry on my walk back home." I start removing items from my cart, placing them randomly on the shelf behind me.

"Hey, you don't have to put your stuff back, I can give you a ride if you need."

"No, I wouldn't want to impose. I can get some of this stuff another day; I just need sheets and a pillow really."

"Consider it a welcoming present. It can stay just between us." With a coy smile I finally accept his request and head to the front of the store to checkout.

"I'll be outside," he says, swiftly exiting the store.

"Okay, thank you for my welcoming gift," I say as he walks away.

He disappears quickly and I locate the nearest register and pay for my items. Once outside the sky seems to have turned completely black with neon lights from nearby stores lighting up the city. Just as my eyes start scanning for Jun Pyo, a sleek blue Acura pulls up to the entrance of the store and he quickly gets out of his car. We move all my stuff into his trunk and get in the car quickly, only silence and the hum of his engine was the audio for our background.

In less than five minutes we are back at my new place. We both sit there still, quiet, and unmoving. Just as I place my hand on the door handle a small photo catches my eye in his compartment. Not wanting to be impolite, but unable to take my eyes off the little boy with big wide eyes is impossible. A woman with high cheekbones and a man that looks exactly like Jun Pyo are holding a baby in their arms.

"That's my family."

"I thought so, you have a beautiful family. Your son is handsome."

"That's actually me," remaining tight lipped his face instantly turns to stone.

"I'm sorry if I've offended you with my question. Sometimes I can be a little too forward."

"No, it's me who is sorry. My family is in North Korea; this is why I responded that way."

Sensing Jun Pyo's pain I decide not to pry anymore and just get the hint that he doesn't want to talk with me, a stranger about his family.

"Well thank you again for your help tonight. I think I can get upstairs by myself."

I don't leave any time for him to respond and hurry to his trunk waiting for it to open. With all my strength I grab my stuff and make the short trek back to my apartment. I struggle to open the door trying to balance everything in my hands. Finally leaning against the metal door, I let everything fall to the floor in one swift motion once inside the apartment.

My thoughts shift back to Jun, my personal nickname for him. Even though I've only been here a day I'm learning about things and people I never could have imagined.

I remember some of my military training focusing on wars from the past. The conflict between North and South Korea all started with an invasion from the North, but even now the conflict was still never resolved. A lot of people from North Korea wanted to flee the country but because of the dictatorship they were trapped. I wonder how Jun came here but not his family. My mind wanders to the way that jacket hung off his shoulders too, but with a loud grumble from my stomach I remember I didn't get any food while I was out.

# Chapter 7

The weekend passed by so quickly with me exploring my neighborhood and learning about the city of Seoul. Although it hasn't been easy getting around, I've managed to feed myself at least properly at the nearby restaurants.

It's finally Monday and I'm excited to get started with the week. My body is still adjusting to the time change and jet lag but even that can't stop my happiness. Not sure what to wear on my first day, I settle on some gray slacks and a white button down with my pointy-toe pumps.

Dak is right on time; I get a text from him notifying me he's outside. Before walking out the door I look in the mirror just one more time ready to pinch myself for this new life I'm living. Even though I've made some choices I regret in the past I just can't fight this feeling that things will be different.

My briefcase in one hand and phone in the other, I jump into the oversized SUV with Dak behind the wheel.

"Good morning, Mav, so how was your first weekend in Seoul?"

"I really enjoyed it; got a few things for the new place, even made a new friend, I actually met one of the agents."

I try to stop myself from saying anything more but it's too late. Dak's face contorts into a confused smile.

"Oh, really and what agent would that be?"

"His name is Jun Pyo, I believe he's one of the agents for South Korea, we'll be working really closely together."

Not even thinking about Jun's simple promise to keep the encounter to myself I think nothing of mentioning my encounter to Dak since I consider him my only other friend here.

"Oh yeah, I've heard of him just be careful around him."

"He seems harmless, I'm sure I'll be okay."

"Let me ask, how much do you know about the last person that was in your job before? Has anyone told you about why this position even opened up so quickly?"

My stomach is in knots wondering why Dak phrased his question like that.

"They told me the department was new, so I didn't think anyone else held the position before. Why? Is there something I should know?"

"Let's just say you should be slow to trust".

His words leave me feeling puzzled and confused but no other explanation is offered.

The car is quiet the rest of the ride to the office. Suddenly the large building feels intimidating with the possibility of knowing something is awry. I thank Dak again for the ride reeling from his comments.

Once I'm finally upstairs I spot Agent Choy at her desk and with a quick wave I make my way towards my new private office. I can't contain my excitement standing in the doorway with my name etched on a sign outside the door.

Once inside, there's a large wooden desk with two small chairs placed in front. Behind the desk is an oversized brown leather chair. I close the door gently wanting to soak up this moment by myself even if it's just for a second. The office looks bare aside from the bulky furniture and three large monitors in the corner of my desk. A small closet is also in the room; I place my belongings inside and get ready for the day.

The day starts out with multiple meetings, and endless surveillance along the borders of North and South Korea. After lunch I check my calendar and see one last meeting with both the American and Korean agents.

A few minutes before the scheduled meeting I follow the other agents to the large conference room I was in a few days ago. Even though there's still about five minutes left before the meeting officially begins the room already looks filled to capacity. I grab one of the chairs furthest away from the large television screen.

A young woman with strawberry blond hair, red lipstick, and a polka dotted dress walks towards the front of the room and suddenly the room grows quiet. Her high cheekbones and thin lips are pursed together until the entire room is focused on her.

"As you all know we have increased our intelligence along the borders in anticipation of an attack. North Korea has been testing out nuclear missiles and they haven't been shy about wanting to attack South Korea. Agent Jun Pyo, what can you tell us?"

Surprised to hear his name, I look up and notice Jun Pyo standing behind the podium to the left of the TV screen. Just like all the other times I've seen him, the first thing that appeals to me are his eyes. Even without staring directly at me he seems to look through everyone in the room. A sleek white shirt and navy pants hang off his body in just the right way. I nibble on my bottom lip hoping to focus on what he's saying and not my raging hormones.

Finally pulling myself from this daydream, I catch the end of what he says ... " as a result of Maverick joining the team, we will coordinate any efforts to find out any upcoming attacks. If you have any new information, please bring it to our attention."

I notice all eyes are on me and I introduce myself again for those I haven't met yet. After a few more moments pass Jun Pyo continues talking, mentioning an operation that will require my team. It's regarding a serious threat that may occur at the Peace Conference gala event to be held in Seoul. Everyone in the office will attend to make sure any officials and dignitaries are safe.

Once the meeting is over, I quickly walk back to my office ready to set up a debrief with my team about the event.

# Chapter 8

Incoming facetime call from Shaunie 1:*00am*

Looking at my phone groggily I contemplate not answering the phone but realize I haven't spoken to Shaunie or anyone for that matter since I arrived in Seoul. I click the accept button to avoid turning on any lights in my dark apartment.

"Wake up!" Shaunie screams, letting her loud voice carry.

"Girl, it's six in the morning over here. I'm sleep," I try my best to sound annoyed but really, I can't contain my excitement. I'm so happy to be speaking with my sister.

"Now don't do that, you know you miss me." Shaunie says.

"I really do sis. It's so crazy over here. The people are actually nice once they stop asking me if I'm Beyonce or some other famous black woman. I got my own office, and they have some good food spots out here."

"I'm so happy for you, living your dreams and doing the damn thing. But girl, in the meantime let me fill you in on what's going on. So, you remember my ex , Jason?"

"You mean Jason, who had two kids and a wife?"

"Yes, his lying ass has been calling me, he even sent a friend request on Facebook. All of a sudden, he is in the process of getting a divorce."

"He did you dirty so why would his divorce have anything to do with you?" The line goes silent and I check my phone screen to make sure our call wasn't disconnected.

"Shaunie… SHAUNIE". Now it's my turn to do the screaming.

"I'm sorry girl. I was just watching this report about this abortion law. You know Texas is making it illegal. They're getting rid of all those over-the-counter pills, and planned parenthood. I really don't know what kind of woman would even have an abortion but sometimes shit happens."

I sit quietly listening to Shaunie feeling like a lump is stuck in my throat. There have been countless times where I wanted to tell her what our mother made me do but I can't. Whether it's from fear or shame, this is a secret only I can hold. What would she think, even more what would my father think. Listening to Shaunie rant about how wrong it is to have an abortion has me thinking back to my own choices and secrets.

After listening to her talk for another five minutes I lie about being tired and needing more sleep. But really, I was looking for any excuse to end the conversation. I'm wide awake and all I can think about is how I wasn't ready in the past to be a mother. How could I bring someone into this world by a man that would never love them? If it was meant to be everything would be perfect like how I see it in my dreams.

A few silent tears slide down my cheeks, but instead of moping in my bed I decided to throw on my workout clothes and go for a light jog to clear my head. I don't care that it's now six-thirty am and that I don't officially have to be up for another hour and a half. Finding solace in lacing a pair of orange Asics sneakers, then after a quick face wash and brushing my teeth I'm out the door.

This is my first time working out since I've gotten here. My usual three-mile run just won't do. I push my body until my muscles ache and finally take a seat on a nearby bench park. All that seems to echo in my head is Shaunie's words: "What kind of woman would get an abortion?"

*Me, that's who.* I'm so lost in my thoughts I don't realize the bench I'm sitting on is in front of a small playground. The sun has risen. No longer does the sky reflect a dark blue. A woman and child are nearby playing on the swings. My heart aches just a little bit more, knowing that when I was presented with the option to have a child and I decided not to.

Now I'm almost thirty with no man, no kids, just a career. Its mornings like this that remind me maybe I focused too much of my life on the wrong things. *Maybe things never had to be perfect to begin with for me to be worthy.*

The little boy decides to jump off his swing midair and his mom catches him in her arms. It's criminal how cute they look, while I'm just sitting here on the brink of a full pity party. Maybe it's my time in the military that made me this way, but I refuse to allow any tears to fall publicly. Even if it's in front of some strangers. I pick up what little pride I have left and decide to cut this workout short, putting my headphones in. I make the trek back to my apartment allowing music to comfort me about past decisions.

# Chapter 9

After last week's debacle of guilt at the park I finally feel like I'm mentally good again. Everything has been going well at work with my team and I've even started having lunch on a regular basis with some of the staff in the office. The gala is coming up next week and even though I know this is just a work event I'm excited to be in the field with everyone. Me and Jun Pyo have been working closely together ensuring agents on our teams are ready to intercept any threats.

The gala will be at one of the biggest buildings in Seoul, Leeum Museum of Art. The property is so large we'll need at least ten drones flying around to listen in on all conversations between possible suspects that want to make an attack. Although most of my night will be spent in our observation headquarters, I'm anxious to be amid all the action. Finally, it feels like I get to prove myself here.

After leading an additional task force meeting about the gala, I grab my things and head towards the elevators while Dak waits outside. We haven't talked much since he gave warning for me to be careful. But since I'm leaving early from work to get my physical done, I think now is the perfect time to try and see what else he knows.

Opening the car door I get in swiftly, not even waiting for Dak to open the door for me like he normally does. We greet each other and jump straight into conversation about Adele's latest album. Dak continues to surprise me saying the new Jasmine Sullivan album is seriously giving Adele a run for her money. I let the conversation flow until we're about five minutes away from the doctor's office. Catching

Dak off guard I ask him more about how he got information on a suspected mole.

"So, Dak, I know we haven't talked much. I wanted to ask what made you suspicious about my position here?

"I'm going to be honest with you, Maverick, I like you so what I'm about to say can't leave this car. This division was created because the first attempt to unify the States and South Korea failed. There was a mole; not sure which side but it was highly suspected they worked for South Korea selling intel and details about certain operations being released. The woman that worked here before you lost everything because she couldn't discover who the mole was. So, when I say be careful, I really mean it."

"Wow. I had no idea. I guess I really do have to keep my eyes open, but why wouldn't they tell me that so I could be on the lookout for the mole, too? It makes sense that they may try to target me."

"Just know that I'm telling you the truth. There have been a lot of attempts to get informants talking but somehow most of them end up dead or back in North Korea. Just take my word for it."

I decide to stop pressing Dak mostly because we are outside my new doctor's office, but I can tell Dak is trying his hardest to keep his mouth shut. But I will find out what's going on with or without his help.

Departing from the truck, I navigate through a large medical building and get ready to meet my new doctor. It's been over a year since my last physical. I'm hopeful everything will be all clear but I feel hesitant to complete the vaginal exam.

After checking in, about ten minutes later I'm being led into an exam room. I change into a medical gown and wait for the doctor to come into the room. A soft knock and in walks a tiny frail woman. Everything but her face seems contorted.

"Hi, I'm Dr. Zhong, nice to meet you... " she pauses and looks down at my chart "Maverick?" she says like it's a question.

"Yes, Maverick Robinson, nice to meet you as well."

"Okay, great dear. Let's get your exam started. I'm going to start with a breast exam and end with examining your pelvis. Could you please lay back on the table and lift your gown and I can examine your breast."

I slowly lift the thin gown up and allow the doctor's cold hands to touch my bare breast. The sensation of her moving her hands between my armpits and left breast forces me to sit as still as possible. After a few minutes she's finally done and allows me to lift the gown back over my chest.

"Thank you, Maverick. Everything feels fine. I don't see any signs of breast growth or anything abnormal. Now we will continue with the pelvic exam. Please continue to lay down and place your feet in the stirrups while I prepare."

Doing as I'm told, the cold metal keeps my legs in place wide open, and my ass is almost hanging off the small bed. She applies a cold gel onto my stomach and presses down feeling around. Once she's satisfied, she reaches for a small medical instrument. She inserts her hands inside me which isn't too bad of a feeling but soon her hands are replaced by the medical clamp. There's intense pressure in between my legs and all I can think about is how I hate coming to the damn doctor.

"Breathe, Ms. Maverick, I promise we're almost done."

I laugh a little at the fact that she can sense my hesitance and finally I relax my body a little more.

"Okay we are finished. Please put your clothes back on and I will be back shortly."

As soon as the door closes, I put all my clothes back on ready to head downstairs, but hear a light knock as I put my last shoe on.

"Ms. Maverick, are you dressed?"

"Yes."

Dr. Zhong walks in, obviously thinking about something.

"Please have a seat Maverick."

"It's okay, I'm comfortable standing."

"I don't know how to say this, but I felt some abnormalities in your uterus. I can't determine anything completely yet as we will need to run further tests. Have you felt any extra pressure in your pelvic, or maybe long menstrual cycles, what about miscarriages?"

"No, I haven't experienced any of that, just slow down. What do you mean you felt abnormalities? What does that even mean?"

"It doesn't mean anything yet, but you may have fibroids in your uterus. We're going to set up an ultrasound to find out more. A woman of your race sometimes has these issues."

"What the hell did you just say? This is all happening way too fast. What do you mean?"

"I don't mean to be offensive; it could mean nothing at all, or it could mean you need to have an operation. Ms. Robinson, having fibroids can show no symptoms at all; it's best to be optimistic until we know more. There is a chance you could have issues getting pregnant in the future, but we need to run more tests first."

"What did you say, does this mean I can't get pregnant, ever?"

"No, it could just be harder to do, listen I don't want to scare you so let's just schedule your follow up appointment so we can find out more."

Dr. Zhong leaves silently allowing me time to grapple with the fact that I may have fibroids. For the second time this week I'm on the brink of breaking down entirely.

Gathering my things, I walk in a dream state back to the front of the office to schedule a follow up appointment. My feet carry me downstairs where Dak is waiting. The sadness in my heart is written all over my face. Dak eyes me suspiciously but doesn't ask any questions, instead he quietly starts the truck and drives me home. All I can manage to do is stare out the window blankly.

Dr. Zhong's words are repeated, "It could be harder." A million thoughts racing in my head but the most prevalent is the belief that I've missed my chance to be someone's mom. It seems like regret has become all that plagues my mind. Will God still choose me, even though I've made decisions in the past about being pregnant.

For the first time since I've gotten here I wish I could just be around my family. I need someone to tell me it's going to be okay and I did the right thing by deciding not to become someone's mom.

I don't know how long it's been since Dak pulled up to my apartment but I manage to tell him to have a goodnight and walk towards the building not bothering to look back even though I hear him calling out my name.

# Chapter 10

A few days later, I'm still a mess over the doctor's news. I haven't had an appetite and have been surviving off ramen noodles and water completely skipping breakfast. My follow-up appointment is today at four pm, apparently there was a last-minute cancellation from another patient. I didn't expect the ultrasound to come up so quickly. I haven't even fully processed that there's something even wrong with me.

I insert some change into the vending machine in our lunchroom, trying to get a grape Milkis. The milk and yogurt soda has become my newest obsession with South Korean culture. I hated them at first but now they've grown on me. I wait for the drink to drop in the slot so I can walk back to my desk, but all I hear is a clicking noise. It sounds like my drink got stuck.

Looking around the lunchroom I see no one's here. I start tapping the machine lightly at first, trying to get my drink and without much notice keep knocking against the machine.

"Hey, are you okay?" Jun Pyo asks.

Surprised to see someone else I quickly say, "Yeah, just trying to get my Milkis, why do you ask?"

"You were banging on the machine; looks you just give it a little love tap," he said.

He proceeds to knock the machine lightly with his side and my drink pops right out, effortlessly.

"Wow, thanks." I abruptly walk off without another word. I'm so lost in my thoughts about this fibroid mess I can't even tell that Jun

Pyo is following me to my office. All I care about right now is being left to my own devices.

"So, you want to tell me what's really going on? You've been avoiding me all week and haven't had any follow-up meetings on my calendar about the gala. I know we haven't talked much about anything outside of work since that night, but really you can tell me what's going on."

"Listen, let's just keep our personal and business separate, I think you made that very clear to me that's how you like to operate. And I haven't scheduled any time on your calendar because I wasn't aware of any updates. My team is prepared. What else should we discuss?"

I know I'm being a little bitchy right now, but again I don't care about anyone else's feelings but my own right now. Jun Pyo's face turns into a hardened shell and any sense of curiosity is erased from his eyes.

"I understand Miss Robinson, well I'll leave you to it and see myself out."

"Okay, do that!"

As the door shuts my tough girl facade crumbles and the tears I've tried desperately to hold escape onto my cheek. I really didn't mean to lash out at him but the way my mouth is set up when I'm mad, I just can't contain my anger. But it's not his fault I'm going through this situation.

I know immediately that I owe him an apology just as I gather the courage to walk to his desk. My meeting reminder pops up, I was supposed to meet with Colonel Davis five minutes ago. Damn.

I gather my laptop and make a quick haste towards his office and try to think of an excuse for my tardiness. I hate being late for anything, I would show up on time to my own funeral if I could.

Lightly knocking on Colonel Davis's door, I hear an abrupt "Come in."

"Hi Colonel Davis, sorry for my tardiness lost track of time." I say vaguely not giving him a real excuse for my tardiness.

"No problem, I was just finishing up a call. I wanted to see how you were adjusting. It's been a few weeks and so far, I have seen you really start taking charge of your team."

"I'm really enjoying myself, sir. Everyone has been really accommodating."

"That's good to hear. Is there anything you have further questions about?"

Something in my gut tells me not to ask the question dying to get out about the mole, but I just can't let it go unasked. I mean it's a valid question that I deserve to know about.

"Sir, I do have one question about what happened to the last lieutenant in this position. I've heard some office gossip about some type of mole that was compromising our missions. Is there any truth to that?"

"Listen lieutenant, I would advise you not to listen to gossip in this building. It's dangerous and repeating it to your superior could cost more than just a conversation. There is no truth to that. We found that the last person in your position just wasn't a good fit, end of story. Am I clear about that?"

"Yes sir, it's crystal clear."

I take mental note of the fact that he never really confirmed if there was a mole or not. Obviously, it's a sensitive situation and if I ask any further questions, I could compromise myself. I let him think I've dropped the subject and wait quietly.

"Great, now regarding the gala you and Agent Jun Pyo have been working together to get ready for. There have been some last-minute changes due to an emergency in Russia. I've asked Agent Jun Pyo to join us so I can notify you both."

As if on cue I hear a light knock on the door and Jun Pyo walks in. His face is still cold and he barely acknowledges me as he greets Colonel Davis and sits down next to me.

"Agent Pyo, thanks for joining us. The reason why I asked you both here is because there have been some last-minute changes to the gala event. Now you're both aware of the recent events in Ukraine and Russia causing some of our resources to be split. Unfortunately, our two main field agents that were set to assist at the gala have been reassigned in Ukraine."

Me and Jun Pyo stare blankly at each other for a moment wondering what this means for our assignment.

"Don't get alarmed, the gala threat is still very real. Our intel has been spot on about some North Korean radicals being at this event looking to harm some very important people. I know this is very last minute, but I was thinking you two could try being in the field."

"I thought we were just doing surveillance," I say.

"Yeah, we are both equipped to monitor, not really be in the middle of everything," Jun Pyo adds.

"Listen, this is an opportunity to level up here, and to be honest this isn't an option. You both know the targets inside and out, no one else can do this on such short notice. I know this isn't what you're expecting but rarely in this line of work are things predictable."

Me and Jun Pyo nod our heads signaling we'll accept. My mind is racing with thoughts of being in the field. I thought an opportunity like this would come after spending more time in Seoul.

"Now that you both are aware I need updates now and someone that can operate as your team lead while you're at the gala. Robinson, who are the high rollers at this event we're expecting to secure?"

Surprised and unprepared, I unlock my computer quickly trying to pull up my notes on the prominent guests. But just as I click on the file a reminder pops up on my calendar reminding me of the ultrasound. Any thought about work ceases, and a silence hangs in the air.

Jun Pyo clears his throat noticeably trying to clear the air he jumps in filling Colonel Davis in on the guests. Reading off names I know but can't quite say as waves of anxiety hit my body. I try my best to look normal and just nod my head along with the conversation.

"Sergeant Robinson..."

"Uhh, yes sir?" I say dazed as Colonel Davis looks at me annoyed.

I try to gauge how long he's been calling my name and look at Jun Pyo, but his face is made of stone again, unable to read.

"I was saying you two will accompany each other. I have prepared a file for the identities you'll assume while at the gala. Now the last thing we need to address is who will lead your teams with surveillance."

"Agent Choy," me and Jun Pyo say in unison and for the first time all day I genuinely smile while adding that Agent Choy has been such a great help in adjusting to my role here. On top of that she knows her shit and can keep both teams in check.

"Okay it's settled. Let your teams know about your decision and let's nail these bastards."

The rest of the afternoon is spent reading the file for my new identity. I'll be portraying Miss Sandy Cutter, a NY Times journalist and Jun Pyo will be my photographer. After alerting my team of the new changes I realize it's past lunchtime and closer to 1:30. My stomach hasn't even grumbled, but I'm pretty sure my stomach is in knots about this appointment later today.

I decide instead of going out for lunch since I'm obviously not hungry I'll opt to stay in my office. I turn down the lights and lock the door, happy that I have actual walls and not glass for someone to see me through like other offices have.

Just as I kick my bare feet up on the small office chaise, I hear a knock. I get up quickly, a little agitated and not bothering to put my heels on. Jun Pyo is standing there.

"I just wanted to make sure we're both squared away with our cover stories?" he asked.

"Yes, I think everything's clear. I am a little nervous about being in the field, but I have always been interested."

"I don't think you'll have anything to be worried about. Once all the men see you in a dress, they'll be too distracted to think about anything else. I know I wouldn't."

"Huh?" I'm slightly taken aback by his comment and get the feeling he was talking about more than work. My lower region gets a little excited at the thought of someone new. But trying to be professional I decide to disregard his comment.

"Yeah, I'm pretty sure you look good in a tux, too," I try giving him a compliment back. My feet are hanging off the chaise bare, with my toes in midair.

I close my eyes hoping he'll get the hint that this is my personal time. He doesn't. In a few moments all I can feel is sheer pleasure as Jun Pyo starts rubbing my feet.

"You have beautiful feet, and strong calf muscles," he says slowly, rubbing his hand closer to my thigh under my tight black skirt.

My eyes are wide open and even though it's wrong, fucking him would be so right. A passion that I haven't seen since he gave me a ride home appears behind his chestnut eyes.

At this point he's damn near on bended knee still only massaging my legs, and damn near having a staring contest with me as we lock eyes.

"I don't think we should do this; someone could come in and see us."

"Well, it's a good thing this door has a lock and that you have a coat closet. I could think of something I need to get while I'm in there."

I know damn well he isn't talking about grabbing a coat; he wants a piece of me. A few thoughts race through my head. I hope he doesn't have a fetish with black girls and that his penis isn't small. I'm not one for stereotyping but that could kill this fantasy. But the loudest thoughts of them all is that my body needs this, fuck the consequences. If I decide to have sex with him I can. Besides, I may not even be able to get pregnant so no need for saving it for Mr. Right. I want Mr. Right Now.

My eyes give him the green light and I'm led to the small coat closet where my jacket is hanging. Jun Pyo is back on his knees pleading with me to lift my skirt up, just as he starts kissing my inner thigh there's a knock on the door.

"Maverick, it's Jin. Can I come in?"

I wipe some drool from my face only to realize I must have dozed off. It was all a dream I thought silently. I unlock the door and continue my day.

# Chapter 11

After having a sexy daydream, I finally feel like my day is getting better. I've even caught up on my assignments and just feel damn good. I know without even looking at the clock it's almost time for my ultrasound appointment. My stomach pangs briefly as nervousness replaces hunger. I know I should feel relieved to go to this appointment so I can learn more about my fibroids, but I know deep down all I really want to do is run away from the possibility that there could be anything wrong with me or my body.

I don't want to believe my chance has already passed to become a mother; I just needed more time. Now that I have my dream job, I just have to find the man I know will be my husband and child's father.

I can't help getting lost in my thoughts. The office is extremely quiet since it's a national holiday today. Mostly everyone has already left the office for the day. I hustle to gather my things and try to make it to my appointment on time. As I round the corner of my office to head to the elevators, I see Jun Pyo doing the same and decide now is the perfect time for an apology.

"Hey Jun, I just wanted to say I'm sorry for the way I spoke to you earlier this morning. I've just been having a rough couple of days and wasn't processing my shit."

"Thanks Maverick, I could tell something was on your mind. It's all in the eyes," he says slightly smiling.

We both grow quiet and just as the elevator doors open, I make a suggestion that will make me skip the ultrasound appointment.

"How about I make it up to you."

"Oh yeah, and how is that?"

"Let me buy you a drink, or multiple drinks if that's what you prefer." I give him my best smile and bat my lashes the way men love so I can get him to say yes.

"Okay, but just one drink."

"One." I say, pointing my finger and smiling mischievously. "Also since I'm still pretty new here could you pick the bar, I kind of thought you might say no so I didn't..."

"No need to explain, I know a place."

After letting Dak know I won't be needing a ride to my appointment, I see it's exactly 4 p.m. Deciding to push the appointment to the back of my mind, I turn my phone off and ride quietly in Jun Pyo's car. The picture of his family sits in the same spot just like before but this time I won't let my big mouth ask any questions about his personal life, at least not yet.

He races through the streets barely missing yellow lights. There is no music and the hum of his engine is the only noise.

Once we arrive at the bar I see it's in a quiet neighborhood not far from the office. At the entrance is a sleek glass door with beautiful koi fish. Peering up, I can see the bar has a small rooftop with a nice view of Seoul. I know immediately this is where we will sit.

Allowing Jun Pyo to park the car I make a quick dash towards the bar ready to drink my way to forgetting about this week. After being greeted by a hostess I ask for seating on the rooftop and walk up some steep stairs with Jun Pyo not far behind.

The wind is blowing lightly and I can feel the sun hitting my skin, making me feel instantly relaxed. I spot a table in the corner of the empty rooftop with a few other people sprinkled in the crowd. I notice a few patrons staring me up and down; guess they are still getting used to seeing a black woman. I don't even care as long as I can get my drink.

"So do you come here often?" I ask while taking in the gorgeous view.

"Every once in a while; it's a really quiet spot."

" I can see that." Looking around I'm reminded that there are only four other people on the rooftop.

The conversation gets quiet again and my eyes are drawn to a small television centered on the wall. Of all the things to be on tv I see a concert for this big K-pop group called BTS. I only know because they play their music everywhere in Seoul. I tap my foot, lightly nodding along to the music that's growing on me just like the city.

The waitress comes back with a bottle of Sake and two glasses. We both thank her and Jun Pyo fills the glasses.

"Cheers to new beginnings and new friends," I raise up my glass and wait for Jun Pyo to lift his glass, too.

With the first shot out of the way, the Sake takes some getting used to. I sit silently but instead of it feeling awkward I'm actually comfortable. Jun Pyo stares off into the sky looking hard to read. Wanting to continue changing the mood I suggest we play a drinking game.

"I know we are coworkers but I think we should get to know each other. I mean pretty soon we'll be in the field together and we'll have to trust each other even more... so why not play a little game?"

"What kind of game?" Jun Pyo stares at me, completely unflinching.

"It's called Answer or Drink."

"Wow. Sounds really creative, but I'm down to play. Let me guess, would you like to go first?"

I can't contain my smile and start with the first question that comes to mind... "When is your birthday?"

****

After countless drinks and questions, we both end up a little tipsy and have to request countless cups of water to sober ourselves up. I ask Jun Pyo if he's okay to drive and try to gauge if he's telling me the truth when he says he'll drop me off at home. Since the sun has gone down the air feels crisp and cold. I hug my arms waiting for the check.

"Are you cold? Would you like to wear my jacket?"

"No, I'm fine; still getting used to the weather here in Seoul." A cold breeze whips through the rooftop and my arms start to shiver from pure reaction alone.

Looking down at my phone, I figure it's safe to turn it back on without being harassed into explaining why I missed the appointment.

"Here, take this," Jun Pyo says.

I look up and see his arm extended, handing me his jacket. His eyes tell me he won't take no for an answer, so I oblige and reach for his jacket.

It's still warm from his body heat and smells of cologne that fills my nostrils. I close my eyes letting the scent get familiar with my senses. It smells so fresh and manly I get lost in this feeling and keep my eyes closed a few more seconds before finally putting the jacket on.

After paying the bill we both exit the bar and head for Jun's car. *Saying Jun Pyo all the time sounds too formal*; I think in my head.

As the car warms up my stomach makes the loudest grumble I've ever heard. I'm so embarrassed; all I can do is stare out the window hoping he didn't hear that noise.

"So should we stop for food?" he smiles and points to my belly.

"Yeah, I guess I am kind of hungry. I didn't have much to eat today. I was so focused on my appointment… I mean work and getting ready for the gala."

"Yeah, me too. There's a street food market not too far from here they have the best mandu."

"Man… what? I'm not so sure about eating food off the street."

"Come on Maverick, live a little. It's called mandu, but you might be familiar with it being called a dumpling. Besides, street food here is just as good if not better than what they sell in restaurants."

I roll my eyes playfully but agree to at least give the food a try. "Fine, but if it's not good you're paying."

"I was paying anyway, It's what a real man does when he's out with a woman."

I laugh a little. What originally started out as an apology feels like it's turned into a date.

The rest of the evening flew by with me trying multiple street dishes. Some were good and others just didn't match my southern American taste buds. We walk the street food market for at least two hours trying food from different stalls. It's amazing to see so many people out this late at night, especially eating food with the different vendors. I still have Jun's jacket on and have to fold the sleeves back just to avoid leaving a stain as I devour the dumplings. Using chopsticks, I roll them around in a sweet orange sauce. He was right; they were good, but they've got nothing on my momma's chicken & dumplings. I lick my lips savoring the last bite of mandu and touch my full belly in satisfaction.

I feel like Cinderella once we finally pull up to my apartment and it's well after midnight. We sit quietly at the front entrance for a few moments. I mostly think about how normally I would be ready to risk it all just for one night of pleasure, but now the reformed Maverick will walk away. Besides, he could just be nice and have no type of desire to be with me in that way.

"Well thanks to a good night, Jun, I really enjoyed myself and couldn't have asked for a better night."

"Me too, you're actually a lot of fun to be around. Make it safely to your apartment. I'll wait till you're in the building to leave."

"Okay, thanks again," I wave goodbye and walk into the building feeling like a giddy schoolgirl.

# Chapter 12

My alarm goes off at exactly 7 am indicating it's time for my morning run. The weather in Seoul is getting increasingly cold so I decide to wear my Nike fleece hoodie and a thermal under my workout leggings.

After quickly brushing my teeth and washing my face I'm ready to start my morning routine. As I scroll through my notifications on the elevator ride down, I notice a few voicemails. Without even guessing I know one message is from the doctor's office. I hit play so I can listen to all the messages.

Once outside I start doing some stretches on a nearby park bench in front of the apartment building, it feels like there's parks everywhere here. As I start stretching my hamstrings, I hear the first message play...

"Hello, we are trying to reach Maverick Robinson," a computerized voice says. "On Friday you missed your ultrasound. Please contact your provider immediately to schedule a follow up appointment."

With no hesitation I delete the message. Without thinking twice, I told myself, *I'll reschedule the appointment just not right now.* I have too much going on with the gala and still getting used to everything here.

The next message is a complete surprise to me. It's my mother. We've been playing phone tag since I arrived in Seoul. I mainly call her at times when I know she and my father are asleep and pretend not to see her messages.

"Hi Mavvy, it's your mom. I want to talk with you and see how your new job is going. Shaunie tells me you've been a little distant and I just want to make sure you're okay. Call me back. I love you."

*Delete.*

My body feels completely warmed up after stretching. I allow my feet to carry me along the park pavement. Although I'm here in Seoul, my mind is somewhere else thinking about the lack of a relationship with my mom. It's not a coincidence that we haven't had a real conversation since I was 17. Somehow all the fears, expectations, and mistakes she made merged into my own. And for that I could never truly trust her, let alone have honest conversation with her.

My mom always thought her daughters' main purpose was to be someone's wife and give her grandbabies and make her proud and carry on tradition, but only if things were perfect. The perfection she sought for our lives was one where you chose a man not just any man, but someone from a good family. A man that never went to jail, didn't have any baby mommas, and a man that was black. She never understood there could be a greater purpose in a woman's life and that relationships didn't have to be perfect to be worth it.

My life doesn't have to be perfect for me to be happy. Every chance she gets I'm reminded that she had it all: a husband, a house, and kids all by the age of 25. It's like I'm a failure in her eyes because I don't have those things. I could have had at least one child by now if it wasn't for her. Pressure to have it all has always been tough on me but it's what I've known to be the expectation.

Before I know it, I'm walking back to my apartment to get ready for the workday.

****

Knock, knock…

"Come in," I say.

Looking up from my screen I see Jun Pyo standing there in gray slacks and a striped button down. I try not to stare too long at him wondering if his cologne will permeate my office.

"Do you have a few moments? I want you to meet Eun Ji, she'll be on board with monitoring for the gala this weekend. I don't think you all have been introduced yet."

"Sure, bring her in." Closing my laptop, I stand up from behind my desk.

Just as I stub my knee against the edge of my desk, I walk past the tallest woman I've seen since I've been here. She towers over my 5'5 frame and looks just as tall as Jun Pyo. Her large, almond shaped eyes light up as Jun Pyo continues telling me about her achievements. Her dark hair is slightly curled. Even though we're in the office, Eun Ji looks like a model.

"So I was filling Eun Ji in about the gala and she'll help in making sure everything runs smoothly with our cover stories."

"Okay, that sounds great. It's nice to meet you," I extend my right hand waiting to shake her hand. She stares at me blankly.

Jun Pyo catches both of our expressions and reminds me that it's tradition to handshake with your left hand.

"Sorry, still getting use to things here," I say to Eun Ji.

"Yes, I can see that," she says smartly.

"Anyway, welcome to the office. Jun Pyo has told me a lot about you."

Eun Ji then lightly grabs Jun Pyo's arm and proceeds to give me the fakest smile ever.

"Well, thank you. Looking forward to working together, if that's all then I have some other things I need to finish before the end of the day," I say flatly.

"Okay, well see you around." Jun Pyo stares at me with so much intensity as he removes Eun Ji's hand from around his arm.

"It's so nice to have some color in the office again, we'll let you get back to work," Eun Ji smiles coyly.

It takes all my strength not to open the door again once it's closed. I can already tell Eun Ji is going to be someone I avoid. Her demeanor and that comment about there being color in the office is enough for me to want to beat her ass. But what really confused me is the fact that she felt comfortable touching Jun Pyo right in front of me, it took him a couple of seconds before he ever removed her hand. Jun Pyo is not my man, but she looked a little too comfortable putting her hands on him.

It's not until almost three in the afternoon when I can finally catch a break from my hectic schedule, noticing I only have thirty minutes to spare until my next briefing.

***

It's almost seven in the evening and I'm still in the office making some final details for expected guests and possible faces to survey during the gala. After typing up some quick notes, I walk to the break room for a quick sip of water, almost all the lights are off as I walk back to my desk all except one. Just as I get closer to the desk, Agent Choy's head pops up from her cubicle.

"Hi Maverick, I didn't know you were still here."

"Yes, just going over some last minute details for this weekend. What are you still doing in the office?" I say leaning against her desk.

"Oh, I'm doing the same. I'm really pleased that you selected me to be one of the surveillance leads. I really don't know how to thank you."

"No thank you needed; I know I've only been here for a short time, but I can tell you're really good at what you do."

"Thank you, that means a lot."

As I prepare to walk back to my office, I hear Agent Choy call my name making me turn around once more.

"Maverick."

"Yes," I say curtly.

"I hope this isn't too personal, but I hadn't seen Dak in a while and was wondering if he was still escorting you?"

"I actually have been slowly learning how to get around on my own, so I haven't needed any rides." Hesitating for a moment, I look around the office before my next sentence. "He mentioned something kind of weird to me, something about a mole being in our department.

Have you heard anything about that? I know you've been here for a while."

All color drains from Agent Choy's face and I could swear she closes something off her screen with the slightest click of her finger.

After clearing her throat a few times, she finally says, "Well yes, there was a mole in the department. It was the last lady that was in your position."

"You mean Colonel Violetta Stone? I looked her up after Dak mentioned she was the one suspected of providing intel that compromised some important missions."

"Yes, you know it was the oddest thing right before she was caught. I think she even tried to point the finger at other agents, but you can't deny the evidence. They checked her emails and sure enough saw enough to fire her and try to put her in jail."

"Really? What other agents did she think could have been working with the mole?"

"I don't really want to say, but she had a big argument with Eun Ji right before she was caught. I don't really know why."

"Okay wow. You're giving me so many more details than Dak. All he's been telling me is to watch my back. But I guess she was the mole. There haven't been any other mistakes since she left."

"I guess so. Whatever you do please don't mention this to anyone. It's a sore subject for everyone in the office. Having a mole who disguised themselves as a friend and coworker. I don't know how we all didn't see it."

"I understand, well thanks for being so honest I'm going to get back to my files. Have a good night, Agent Choy."

Once back in my office I think about all the new information I have and what to do with it. I unlock my phone and start texting Dak to let him know that Violetta was the mole but thinking about what Agent Choy said, instead of hitting send I just hit delete. I get back to work thinking this mole situation can be put to rest.

I sift through a few file folders on my computer until I finally locate exactly what I'm looking for. Before clicking DELETE on my folder with intel on the mole I open some of the files again.

The first is a short description about Violetta Stone, she was in the air force for fifteen years and only held the position in Seoul for eight months. She had no husband, barely any family except a younger brother, and worked closely with the Latin American division prior to being transferred to Seoul. Up until her time here she always had high remarks from other officers and never even got in trouble. Her record was as clean as a whistle; even now looking at her service picture she doesn't look like the type to reveal government secrets. But these days you never really know what people are capable of.

After looking over a few more stats about Violetta, I open an article mentioning how Violetta could be charged with treason. She was never sentenced for anything officially, but the military has a way of getting their own justice one way or another. The last sentence says Violetta is awaiting trial in her hometown and lost any credibility to continue her career. Once she was fired, all the other files for projects she was working on became redacted with black marks striked through.

The only thing I could find was her last case involving some unnamed diplomat. Apparently, his family in North Korea was attempting to flee. The mystery man was willing to provide intel about nuclear threats and defense plans.

Unfortunately, due to surveillance issues with the drones the team lost sight of the contact and his family. Exactly three weeks later the informant and his family were reported as dead and immediately after Violetta was discovered to be leaking information.

As I mentally debate whether I should believe Dak or Agent Choy I click on the folder.

*DELETE.*

# Chapter 13

I twist my hair to the right like I see the girl do on YouTube but instead of my hair looking like hers it's a kinky mess. Ever since I took my knotless braids out, I haven't been able to get my hair to tame itself. I rewind the YouTube tutorial for the fifth time trying to get my hair to look like the girls on my screen. Again, instead of the front of my hair forming the perfect front twist it looks bunched up. Growing frustrated, I call the only person I know that can help.

"Siri call Shaunie."

The phone rings a few times before I finally hear Shaunie's voice.

"Well, if it isn't my long lost sister."

"Hey Shaunie," I say light heartedly catching on to her no-nonsense tone of voice. "Sis, I need your help."

"First off, why are you treating me how you treat your mama avoiding my calls and shit? Ever since that abortion conversation you been ducking my calls, why is that?"

I pause before thinking of an excuse to try to avoid her question.

"What do you mean, I've just been really busy with this gala event which is why I called you for help."

"Bullshit Mav, I don't know why you always try to avoid shit like I don't know your ass. Let's be real. I said something that hurt your feelings and you don't know how to address it to me."

"Why would you think you hurt my feelings Shaunie? Like I told you I've been busy."

"Okay Mav, if that's the case then why did I find an empty abortion pill packet at your apartment in Houston?"

My heart instantly plummets into my stomach and my mouth goes desert dry. *How would Shaunie even know about that?* A few words stumble out of my mouth trying to form a coherent sentence.

"I... "I'm not sure what you're talking about, honestly."

"So, remember when we spent that last night in your place before you left, when I asked to use your purple headband? Well, when I went to look for it in the bathroom, I found the pills."

"Oh, so now you're snooping through my drawers being nosey Shaunie." I say a little louder than I expected.

"I wasn't snooping but anyway you never told me you were even pregnant, but now it all makes sense why you were acting so quiet on the phone. Then you hung up on me." Her turn to pause. "I just don't know why you would do something like this."

"You know what Shaunie this is exactly why I didn't tell you, because I knew you would be judgmental. It's not anyone's business but my own and I made the best decision for me. So, what if you don't understand."

"Judgmental? Girl you're one to talk. Is this the same sister that looked at me strangely because you found out I was sleeping with a married man."

"This is different Shaunie, and you know it. It doesn't affect anyone but me. Unlike you who messed with that man even after you found out, what about his family?"

"Whatever Mav. Tell me this, do you even regret what you did? I mean at the end of the day you didn't even consider the life growing inside of you, and what about the father? Did you even tell him?"

"Like I said this really isn't something I want to talk about with you. It was my choice not to continue the pregnancy. It was what was best for me."

"I think it was selfish, but why am I not surprised? That's who you are and always have been. What would Mom think if I told her, you did some shit like this?"

"Bye Shaunie."

I click END on my phone so fast I almost accidentally call her back. Looking in the mirror with my hair looking a mess and my nostrils flared from anger all I can see is red. I can't believe Shaunie knew. This was a secret I planned on adding to my already full closet of skeletons. And for her to mention my mother? She doesn't even know our mom would probably applaud me for what I did.

Allowing my anger to subside after taking a few deep breaths I think of the other shit Shaunie said. She called me selfish and judgmental but has the nerve to judge me on a decision I made. And sleeping with a married man is better?

After deciding that I won't call Shaunie back I take one last fleeting look at my hair and decide I can't do this alone. I pick up my phone and start typing expecting some small miracle.

I type in the search bar "black hair stylist near me" and two shops pop up nearby. The first one is called Noni's; it's only a fifteen-minute walk and even has accompanying pictures of the different hair styles they do. The second shop is called Kink and it's about thirty minutes away and has really good reviews.

I decide to try Kink and take the train to save time scrolling through their website. I settle on Marley twists instead of my signature box braids and with one swift move head out the door.

I open the door to Kink thirty-five minutes later, pleasantly surprised to see two black women standing behind chairs with their hands full of braiding hair. I breathe a huge sigh of relief as a young Asian woman working the front desk asks me what kind of style I want.

"Yes, I would like to get my hair done with the Marley locs."

"Okay, Patricia should be finished in the next thirty minutes with her client. You can take a seat over there," she says, pointing to a small waiting area near the entrance.

I take the seat closest to the door and notice the knee-length table has a few magazines scattered on the clear glass top. I spot Essence magazine with Chloe and Halle Bailey on the cover. They are always so versatile but, on the cover, they are proudly displaying the locs on their crown. Reclining into the chair I flip through the next few pages feeling a sense of relief come over me. It actually feels like I'm at home in the small salon inhaling the fresh scent of hair grease and the hum of a blow dryer.

"Excuse me, Maverick. I'm Patricia we can get started with your hair now."

Looking up from the magazine I'm able to get a better look at Patricia. She has an auburn lace wig that matches her tan skin and freckles. Glancing at the door I see the woman that was sitting in her chair exit.

"Wow that was quick. Okay where do I go?" I ask.

After a good wash and blow dry my hair is finally ready to have the Marley braids installed. Since I didn't bring any hair, I use what they have on hand.

Patricia walks from a small back room with two packs of hair: one 4A jet black which is my color, but she has a purple pack of hair in her other hand. I'm not really used to having color in my hairstyles. *Another result of my military lifestyle.*

"Patricia, do you have any more of the 4A color?"

"Afraid not, these are our last two packs in the store. Believe it or not we have a lot of clients requesting this style."

I look around puzzled and whisper, "But there aren't that many black women here."

She gauges my face for a few seconds before having a fit of laughter like I've just told the world's funniest joke. As she starts parting my hair she says slowly, "Well, out here black people aren't the only ones exploring new things."

She gives me a wink and as if on cue a young Asian lady walks to the front of the shop with knotless braids to her ass coming from the same room Patricia was just in.

"Oh, I understand now."

I quietly observe the lady with the braids seeing her hips shift from one side to the next. There's a thick coat of gel applied to her edges to make it look like she has baby hair, too. I can't look at her hair and mannerisms without thinking of cultural appropriation, but instead of addressing it to Patricia I just unlock my phone to scroll through Instagram and wait for her to work her magic.

After four hours my hair is finally done and I'm honestly pleased.

"I really love my hair Patricia. This looks really good. Thanks for putting the purple hair on the bottom."

The large mirror placed in front of her station allows me to admire my hair from every angle. "I should be able to blend it in so it won't be so obvious."

"No problem sweetie, just make sure you come back once you're ready for something different. I know what it's like working in corporate America. You have to blend in."

Not bothering to correct her about what type of job I have, all I can do is smile as I hand her a couple won bills with the tip included.

"I will definitely be back, thanks Patricia."

After stepping out of the salon headed back toward the train station, all I can do is smile. I was so worried about moving to Seoul because I thought there wouldn't be anything for me here. But after trying new food and exploring the city by myself I really feel like I made the right decision. Even getting my hair done was something I was dreading but I realized I was stressing over nothing. Entering the underground train station, I allow my happiness to radiate to every person I pass. *Today will be a good day.*

***

Staring at myself in my bathroom mirror I apply a light shade of plum MAC lip gloss and admire my makeup. The YouTube makeup tutorial turned out better than it did with my hair. After applying some light foundation to my face and using some gold eyeshadow to accentuate my eyes I feel like I'm ready to step out the door.

Glancing at my phone as I apply a little more mascara, I notice I've got about twenty more minutes before Dak picks me up. We haven't talked much which I know is a result of my doing. I've avoided his texts and request to continue being my driver even though it's considered a part of his job. For some reason I just can't shake the feeling that he's overthinking the mole situation. I hope he doesn't mention it on the ride over to the gala.

My bare feet tread against the wood floor towards my laptop and decorative gold heels on the seat cushion of my black leather couch.

After unlocking my computer, I take one final look at my folder details about my new identity. My name for tonight is Sandy Cutter, a journalist from the NY Times covering the World Peace Gala. The Leeum Museum of Art is a huge space taking over thirty acres of space with large art displays and exhibits from artists around the world. It's so expansive it takes over two hours to walk the entire property. It's the perfect cover to use the drones and keep an eye out for any upcoming threats. As part of my story, I'll be getting opinions about relations between the US and South Korea from a few key players in the government in Seoul. Jun Pyo will record the media which will serve as additional surveillance and allow us both to act quickly if we perceive any threats.

My alarm goes off at exactly 8:00. It's officially time for the biggest night of my career to begin just like that. I close my laptop and slowly lean down to strap my heels against my ankle. As if on cue a text from Dak appears on my screen just as I practice walking with my heels on.

*8:02pm* : Downstairs

Walking out of the lobby entrance I spot the dark sedan parked to the right of the lobby entrance and slowly strut towards the car. Approaching the car swiftly Dak appears instantly and opens my door. His eyes bulge at the sight of me with his jaw damn near hitting the floor.

"Wow! Maverick you look beautiful!" he says in his thick British accent.

I melt into the leather seats as my dress hugs the seat cushion "Thanks Dak you're not too shabby yourself," admiring his gray striped suit and fresh haircut.

I take a real look at Dak. He has a strong nose and sparkling white teeth. If I didn't work with him maybe, just maybe, I'd fuck him.

"It's been a while since we last saw each other. How have you been getting around?"

"Oh, I've been taking the train or just walking. I have to say it's been nice experiencing the city. I've learned a lot about how things work here."

"Well, that's great to hear, although I won't lie I do miss our rides especially our music sessions on the way in. My current services are with someone who just hates any noise at all in the car. Shit, I can't even sneeze without getting the side eye."

Laughing instantly at the sight of Dak trying to stay quiet for an entire ride I ask, "So who is this person that just loves to be in a constant state of quiet?" half expecting him to answer.

"Oh, it's the ice queen, Ms. Eun Ji. She really doesn't have clearance for this service but somebody put in a special request for her to have access to a driver and transport. She really just glares at me when she thinks I'm focused on the road and types on that little laptop of hers."

My stomach tightens in instant aggravation and with just the mention of her name my eyes roll.

Dak, not missing a step, reads my body language through the rearview mirror and says, "I take it you don't get along with Little Miss Sunshine either?"

"You would be right." I got into a description of the recent encounters I'd had with Eun Ji and her weird behavior. I conveniently leave out the way she was feeling Jun Pyo up. We both talk back and forth about how Eun Ji behaves and some of the blatant racist comments she makes.

Me and Dak's conversation flows as swiftly as a tennis ball in a match, each of us taking our time to vent. Before I know it, we're driving up to a secluded long driveway just yards away from the Leeum Museum.

"It's showtime. Good luck Mav."

"Thanks Dak, you too."

Watching as the taillights of the sedan disappear down the never-ending driveway, I walk to a small stone building that could easily be confused for a garage. I knock lightly on the wooden door ready to get briefed. The door opens slightly, and Agent Choy peaks her head between the space as she recognizes me. The door is opened completely.

"Wow, Maverick you look different..." she pauses awkwardly.

I'm not sure if I should be insulted or flattered but she quickly regains her composure.

"I just mean you look different outside your work clothes, but you look amazing." I admire the way her dark red gown hangs on her as well.

"Thanks Choy. Well, let's get started. Let me know how things are looking. Any sightings of our guests at the party yet?" I ask, referring to the list of potential terrorist and militia organizations.

As we continue talking, I see Agent Eun Ji walk by. She snidely stops and looks at me. "Maverick, I didn't notice you there."

As she walks closer to me, I could swear I look like some kind of experiment to her. The way her eyes open wide and her mouth is hanging open.

"Interesting hair; can I touch it?"

Her hand reaches out to touch my locs but quickly moving out of her reach I avoid her hands.

"Look Agent Eun Ji, don't touch my hair. We need everyone focused tonight and that includes you even though you're just here for show. Now please go follow up with your lead to confirm where you should be, because it's definitely not here."

I wait for Eun Ji to walk away letting her know she can't have access to me or my hair. Agent Choy continues.

"As I was saying, the guests we're looking for haven't arrived yet. But there is something that needs your attention. One of Violetta Stone's contact's is here, a Darcelle Ramirez. She has some ties to the South American government and was one of the only people who defended Stone. Might be a good idea to keep an eye on her in case she tries something."

"Great Choy, I'd definitely be interested in keeping surveillance on her. Where is Agent Jun Pyo?"

"He's just through those doors," she says pointing straight back to a set of oversized wooden doors with brass handles.

As I walk towards the back of the building, I say hello to a string of other agents. I lightly knock on the door and grab the brass handle slowly. What I see once the door is open damn near makes me choke.

Jun Pyo is standing there dressed in a tall black suit with a purple tie. His normally cold eyes meet mine and seem as warm as a fireplace in Vermont on a cold night. Instead of his hair being tame tonight it's a little wilder shielding his cheeks and face.

We both smile at each other with a familiar sense of comfort in the air.

"So, I guess you got the memo about wearing purple too, right?" I ask.

"I guess you could say that I've never seen you look like this before, there's something different about you tonight."

"There is? Well, I'll take that as a compliment. It seems like you're not the only one who thinks I don't look like myself," I say arrogantly before laughing at my own comment.

He chuckles and slightly readjusts his pants. If I didn't know any better, I would say he's a little hard based on that bulge. Instead of focusing on my personal thoughts I jump straight into the events of the gala.

Over the course of the next hour me and Jun Pyo review our team's assignments and make sure every part of our operation is perfect. At last, the event is finally starting as I see a large light come to life up near the museum. It cuts through the darkness in the window of the small stone building.

"Is everyone in place?" I ask, testing out my mic which was placed in the small of my ear hidden by my hair.

A cohesive "yes" erupts from the listening device and a final signal to head to the gala is made.

"Okay team, let's work together to make sure this event ends the same way it started, quietly and safely."

# Chapter 14

I enter the media entrance through a side door to the massive building made out of white bricks with Jun Pyo not far behind with a camera on his left shoulder. We might as well be invisible to the sea of leaders parading through the gala. A crowd of dignitaries walk past us and I swear I see the princess of Cameroon in the center.

My eyes can't seem to capture everything in the large room from the floor to ceiling curtains framing the tall windows. Over half the room is filled with oversized round tables with crystal centerpieces and a pink flower I've learned to be called the Mugunghwa, Seoul's national flower. Everything is so elegant and beautiful. There's even an art display showcased in an adjoining room with photographs of the history of Seoul.

The party is just starting as more guests arrive wearing outrageous displays of fashion. If I didn't know any better I would think I was at the Met Gala. Among the crowd are faces from almost any realm of the earth here for the Peace Conference.

After doing an observation of the perimeter, I instruct Agent Choy to begin operating the drones. A few seconds later I hear the familiar buzz of the machine hovering nearby. As I turn around to face Jun Pyo I notice his eyes move upward to my face which I know were previously settled on my ass.

He clears his throat for the second time tonight before speaking.

"Uhmm...so shall we get started with some interviews? I see the Prime minister of England over there." He points directly across the room to Carter Flemming, a man no taller than 5'5 with a toupee on his head.

"Okay, let's begin. I think it'll be interesting to get some feedback from him about the recent attacks and how they can be prevented."

"Great, you lead the way, Sandy," Jun Pyo says.

***

It's been at least one full hour since the party has started and so far all I've been able to intercept are side eyes from a few women that act like they've never seen a black woman before. I signal for Jun Pyo to come closer.

"Hey, I'm going to freshen up I'll be back in a few."

Walking towards the women's restroom I continue to scan the room. As I pull the door someone on the other side pushes and there's this weird exchange as we both try to repeat the action again. I let go of the door and on the other side is Darcelle Ramirez.

She's strikingly beautiful just like the picture Choy showed me earlier. Her hair is bone straight and her light caramel skin has not a blemish in sight, with cat-like eyes and a thick Brazilian accent she says, "Excuse me."

She's wearing an emerald green dress with a silver necklace that dips low to her waist. She stares at me a second too long but I proceed inside the restroom. Once in the stall I advise Agent Choy to follow Darcelle until I'm finished.

After clearing my bladder at an impeccable pace and washing my hands, I rush out of the restroom looking to find Darcelle.

"Agent Choy, give me Darcell's location. I think I need to have a chat with our friend."

"All clear, she's standing on the patio adjacent to the band."

"Thanks, and Jun Pyo give me a few minutes to speak to her, alone."

"All clear, Mav."

Covertly walking to the other side of the massive room I walk outside to the large brick patio that's just as lively as the inside of the gala. A long Olympic-sized pool reflects the moonlight and enhances the beauty of this night.

I spot Darcelle after a few minutes of searching the crowd standing off to the side with champagne in her hand. An irritated glare rests on her face making her seem unapproachable.

After clearing my throat and straightening my back, I walk slowly over to her. In my most professional voice I make my entrance standing directly in front of her ready to make small talk.

"It looks like you're enjoying this just as much as I am." I smile as genuinely as I can and wait for her hard features to soften.

"Believe it or not I'm actually here to meet an old friend, that at this point is standing me up," she says looking at her Movado watch.

"What do you say we pass the time together until your friend arrives?"

"I'd say you've got a deal, and just what do you do Ms... I didn't even ask your name?"

A waiter passes by with champagne and Darcelle quickly replaces her glass and grabs one for me. Offering it to me as some sort of prized possession, I decline.

"My name is Sandy Cutter, with the NY Times. I appreciate the offer. I'm on the clock," pointing to the phony press pass I have around my neck."

"Oh shit, you're with the press? Maybe I should wait alone?" she laughs, drinking the first flute of champagne quickly and placing it on the edge of the table nearby.

"We're not that bad, I promise anything you say to me is off the record."

"Is that so? Well aside from peace what are you covering tonight?"

"I have been trying to figure out some details about the drone intelligence program here in South Korea. I've been having the hardest time following up with a potential lead, by the name of Violetta Stone. Maybe you know her?" I say bluntly.

Her eyes close into tiny slits and the champagne glass rises to her lips with one large gulp she finishes the drink off. Darcelle's body language shifts and her arms cross against her chest there is no sign of the smile that rested on her face a few seconds ago.

Not allowing my comments to spook her I quickly say, "Listen Darcelle, I'm an investigative journalist. I've heard about Violetta's story and I know that you two were on the same committee during her time here in Seoul. Do you have any comments about your colleague and her actions against her country?"

She looks at me puzzled with her upper lip scrunched up "Listen, Ms. New York Times, Violetta did nothing wrong except trust those people at her job. And not that it's you or anyone else's business but she is innocent," Darcelle says angrily with her nostrils flared.

"I can tell I've made you upset. I'm sorry it's just puzzling to think she has compromised rescue missions of people trying to escape North Korea?"

"How would you know what type of compromises she made? You really can't believe everything you read in the papers, Ms. Cutter."

Her face continues to be inflamed with anger. Taking a step closer to me she says in a hushed voice, "If I were you I wouldn't go around loosely mentioning these accusations. The last person that started asking questions ended up being framed."

A chill runs up my spine the way she says the word *framed*, and all I can do is look into her eyes as they taunt me.

"And to think I was looking forward to not going to my hotel room alone. You take care, Ms. Cutter."

Darcelle spins around angrily but before I can let her walk off in the opposite direction I jump in front of her unexpectedly catching her off guard.

"If it wasn't Violetta, then who?"

"That's for you to find out, 'investigative journalist'," she says, making air quotes with her fingers "But if I were you, I'd start with the people she worked with."

With a sense of finality, Darcelle walks away leaving me just as confused as I was before this conversation. Before I have enough time to mentally process the conversation Jun Pyo is walking towards me with an alarmed expression.

"Is everything okay? I saw you talking with that woman."

"Yes, just following up on a lead," I say dismissively.

A concerned glance still rests on his face but getting the hint that I don't want to talk about it Jun Pyo proceeds with letting me know of the guests that have arrived.

We both quietly enter the building again stopping in the area reserved for the press. Jun Pyo places the camera in a chair nearby as he surveys the room. Just as I tap Jun Pyo to walk towards another guest for questioning I see something strange out of the corner of my eye.

Darcelle has a glass of champagne in her hands and standing next to her of all people is Dak. I can't fathom what those two have to talk about and can't even form any words as Jun Pyo tries to ask me what I want. All I can do is stare across the room. It's unnerving how familiar the two look with Darcelle's hand wrapped around Dak's fore-arm. It should be criminal how I'm staring them down, and Jun Pyo follows my trained eye.

"Isn't that your driver?" Jun Pyo asks.

"Mmm hmm."

My mind is racing with a million thoughts mainly how Dak failed to mention he would be attending the gala as a guest.

"I'm surprised to see him here," I say, still in awe of what I'm seeing. It's as if Dak knows I'm staring at him and his eyes pierce into mine as he looks from me to Darcelle. His stature frame is standing at full attention and within an instant I see him walking towards us. Not quite ready to talk to him, I grab Jun Pyo's arm quickly and surprise myself by saying, "Let's dance."

I refuse his futile attempts to say no and stop me and instead head to the large dance floor currently full as a rendition of John Coltrane's "Favorite Things" is played by the band. I stare in Dak's direction and his face reads a hint of sadness. A young couple dances slowly in front of him, restricting his ability to walk towards us.

Not missing a beat I place my form fitting arms around Jun Pyo's shoulder and wait for his hands to settle on my waist. My heart seems to be linked with his as we sway to the sound of the jazz. I don't know if the band or my heart is playing the loudest in my ears. For only a moment I forget about everyone else in the room and just relish in the warmth of being in a man's arms.

"Are you sure you're alright? I think your driver is trying to get your attention," Jun Pyo says, spinning me slightly as Dak draws nearer cutting through the thick crowd.

Instead of responding I draw closer to him; too close as my breast crushes against his broad shirt. I feel my nipples harden from the friction as we continue swaying. Our feet move in some sort of weird two-step as we inch further away from Dak.

I stare up into Jun Pyo's chestnut eyes that hold so much emotion yet no words are exchanged between us. If he had been anyone else I would've fucked him already but I was giving myself an honest chance to not mix business with pleasure. As I start to feel my emotions shift towards something romantic, Jun Pyo pulls away suddenly looking like he's done something wrong. I don't know if he feels the heat pulsating from my body to him but I don't try locking my arms to his shoulders again but instead slowly take a step back giving us some space.

The motion seems futile as I feel a new pulse beating down below my waist, the type of yearning that can only be fulfilled in one way. I touch my ear lightly as I adjust my ear piece. I turn around facing the crowd and see Dak is within an arm's length distance. My view is obstructed slightly so I move further away from Jun Pyo and Dak who's on my heels.

"Maverick, can we talk please?" Dak asks, his voice above a whisper and hand lightly grabbing my elbow.

"I'm sorry, I can't right now," I say being short with him.

Jun Pyo's jaw tenses staring at Dak's hand but he dare not say anything trying to gauge my reaction.

My eyes move upward as I hear the familiar buzz of a drone nearby, but instead the eye in the sky being one of our drones trained to only take pictures of the event I have to damn near blink a few times.

I urgently whisper, "Who authorized a black sky quad to be in the air?

I hear Agent Choy respond quickly "We don't have a record of that type of drone being flown by any agents tonight."

"Get that drone out of the sky now," I say a little louder than expected.

My feet start towards a side exit in the direction of the control room. As I reach the edge of the dance floor with Dak close behind, my heart drops at the sound of gunshots ringing out.

Screaming into my ear piece I try to let my team know the rogue drone firing shots needs to be taken down. I also hear at least five other conversations happening as everyone scrambles to give out orders. I can't see Jun Pyo but hear his voice through the earpiece saying something in Korean I can't quite understand.

The party is in full chaos as the once elegant building is now being bombarded by mobs of people trying to exit. The sultry jazz has been replaced by screams and panic as guests start scrambling every way to avoid danger.

I don't have time to go back for Jun Pyo but Dak is right behind me. The drone sounds like it's hovering right above my head as I try my best to not get trampled over. My dress gets caught on a nearby leg chair. Dak helps me lift the long dress up from the chair's leg.

Just when I think we're safe I hear another loud shot as if the bullets firing have my name on it. I keep moving but hear a loud animal-like scream. Turning around I see Dak has been hit. His body is sprawled over a table and crimson blood stains his white dress shirt. I turn back around and race to him not sure if he's dead or alive.

"Dak, can you hear me?" I run to his aid and try to lay his body flat down near the table.

"Hell no! I've been shot!" he says trying to give me a light smile that never reaches his eyes.

"Let me just take a look," I examine the area where the blood is on his shirt unbuttoning the area near the stain. I see a wound right below his ribcage as Dak tries to sit up. I push his body back down not wanting him to strain his body any more than it already is.

My head spins and the internal alarm of danger rings painfully loud as I search the room more frantically looking for help. I cover the wound with my hands trying to apply pressure and within an instant me and Jun Pyo's eyes lock across the room like he heard my cry for help. He runs to me alarmed at all the blood now on my dress.

"Maverick, are you hit?" he asks, looking concerned.

"No, it's Dak. He was hit in the ribcage," I explain, lightly lifting my hand to show the wound. "Please send help. I don't know how long he has."

I yell Dak's name too many times to count but he has stopped responding with his eyes closed all I can do is hold onto him.

"It's going to be okay," Jun Pyo says, bending down to level his body with mine. He wipes my face with his thumb. I jump back surprised, not even aware of the tears sliding down my face as he puts his fingers around my shoulder instead.

"You're shaking, Maverick. I promise everything will be okay. Please trust me," Jun Pyo says trying to keep me calm.

I can't pull myself to say anything but his words put me at ease and I try to get a hold of myself while we wait for help. My mind feels numb with regret for avoiding Dak and him being so close to me. All I can think about is that bullet may have had my name on it but it was in Dak's body.

# Chapter 15

The ambulance speeds away with loud sirens in the night air. Dak is still unconscious. Everything around me is muted with only thoughts of Dak surviving catching my attention.

Agent Choy's lips are moving but I can't seem to respond. Jun Pyo takes the lead like he always does when I'm incapable of pulling myself together. He explains the series of events that led up to the drone attack and Dak being shot. Our team looks on in horror as I grab at my dress which now has a large blood stain right above my waist.

The drone has been disabled and the remnants of the extravagant gala are gone. The only people left on the property are security personnel. As if snapping out of some sort of trance I force myself to pay attention to what's being discussed.

"Maverick, I'm going to drive you home," Jun Pyo says.

"Okay," is all I can say but the thought of spending the night alone with my thoughts seems just as frightening as this night.

Eun Ji appears from the shadows with her mouth sneered ready to say something slick.

"Jun Pyo, I'm sure we can arrange for someone else to drive her home. Perhaps another driver that can take Dak's place?"

Normally I would respond to her open disrespect towards me but not tonight, not right now.

Instead of giving her what she deserves I just stand there still shaken up.

"Eun Ji, I think it's time you head back to the meeting point with the others," Jun Pyo says coming to my defense again tonight.

Eun Ji raises her eyebrows in annoyance before exhaling loudly and mumbling under her breath in Korean.

After a few more minutes I follow Jun Pyo to his car as we walk back to the long winding driveway I saw when first arriving. I spot his car a few steps away from the stone building. He already has the passenger door open for me patiently waiting until I'm inside to close the door. I take my time securing my seatbelt replaying the last hour of the party in my mind like some slow motion movie scene.

The shots ringing in the air like twisted music, all the blood on my dress, and my first covert mission turned into a failure. I couldn't protect anyone tonight, not even myself. The confidence I had about tonight being successful continues to deflate as I overhear Jun Pyo's call. There were apparently more casualties including a foreign official. I sink further into the seat wishing I could just disappear.

*** 

It seems like seconds instead of minutes as Jun Pyo pulls up to my apartment with the engine idling. Jun Pyo breaks the silence between us.

"Maverick, would you like me to walk you up?"

"No," I say a little too quickly.

"Okay, I understand if you need a few more minutes," his hands grip the steering wheel awkwardly like he's unsure of what else to say.

"No, I mean I don't want to go upstairs. I don't think I should be alone right now."

"Oh, is there someone I can call for you?" he says innocently.

"I don't have anyone," if only he knew all the people that get close to me end up being pushed away.

The idea of calling Shaunie makes me contort my face. I am not ready to speak with her yet. I grab Jun Pyo's hand on the steering wheel and look at him desperately feeling like I need his touch to calm me.

"I just need to be with someone tonight that I trust."

" I know a place," he says, removing my fingers from his and shifting the car into drive.

After riding for another forty minutes we pull up to a secluded brick home with a privacy fence surrounding the yard. This is my first time outside the city and it's completely different than what I've gotten used to. Not asking any questions I assume this is Jun Pyo's house from the way he punches in the security code opening a small gate. I'm pleasantly surprised by the size of the house as we drive through the gate. I figured he would live in an apartment like me but this house is quite the opposite of my living conditions.

Once inside I have a clear view of the yard which has a small pond, a wooden bench, and flowers creating a narrow path to the front door. The gravel in the yard crunches with each step of my heels. The air feels better out here as I inhale the scent of grass and hear crickets chirping in the distance.

I stand behind Jun Pyo as he unlocks the canary yellow door allowing us to enter the house.

"Maverick, please come in, this is my home."

In the entryway he turns on a few lights and disappears quickly out of my sight. I lean on the doorway nearby and stay close to the front of the house. I bend down slightly wanting to free my feet from the now uncomfortable heels. It's a miracle they didn't come off from all the commotion earlier. In what feels like forever, I breathe a deep sigh of relief knowing I'm safe.

Staring down at my dress I realize it would have been smart to grab some of my own clothes from my place. Unsure where to look for Jun Pyo, I walk further into a spacious living room. A small couch low to the floor sits in the middle of the room. There's a fireplace with a stone mantle set atop the stone is a picture of Jun Pyo's family, the same one he keeps in his car. I rub my hands on the smooth stone letting my fingers become familiar as I hear footsteps approaching.

"I thought you could use a change of clothes."

I turn around and see Jun Pyo standing with an oversized t-shirt and sweatpants in his hands. I swear this man can read my mind in some weird way.

After saying thank you Jun Pyo shows me where I'll be sleeping. A guest bedroom adjacent to what I assume is his room has a small light on. I quickly walk past the door ready to get in the guest room and wash this day away.

Once I'm alone, the darkness of the night fogs my brain. I peel the dress off slowly right in the middle of the room letting it fall to the soft carpet. The red stains look so foreign on the gown that even without looking at the blood directly I know this dress will never be worn again. A few specks of blood adorn my wrists and guilt creeps into my veins.

If I hadn't have been avoiding Dak, maybe he wouldn't have got shot, I wonder what he wanted to tell me. I know if he wasn't near me that bullet would have hit me and not him.

I set the water on hell. Wallowing in my self-pity, I step into the shower with thoughts as foggy as the steam building up in the bathroom. The water gives my skin a burning sensation at first but I don't flinch from the sensation. I welcome the temporary pain of feeling my skin boil from each drop of water. The dried off blood on my arms falls off my body and swirls down the drain.

My mind is like an open gate that can't be closed tonight and another type of guilt takes over. No longer strong enough to stand, I sit on the tub bare just like my thoughts. I feel guilt for my decision to be selfish in every aspect of my life. I used to tell myself I was selfish because I wasn't ready but I know the real reason. My ability to shut people out isn't normal, but it's all I know.

Tonight my selfishness could have cost Dak his life; another innocent person I can say I've ruined. He's not the first innocent life I feel responsible for. I could have been a mother by now but instead all I am is alone. Up until now I never had to hold myself accountable. It's like I passed the blame onto everyone else. Lawrence was a walking red flag and I let him in again when I should have just controlled myself.

My sister knows my deepest secret about the abortions and now I could be in jeopardy of even having a child in the future. I'm a failure at love, being a good sister and friend.

My heart aches and depression fills my head inflating as each minute passes. I try to hold the urge to cry building in my throat and focus instead on the cascade of water from the shower head. But what I feel right now seems to plague me mentally and physically.

I gasp for air and know what's coming next, a panic attack. I try to breathe through my nose and mouth in concentrated breaths. It's been years since I had an attack like this. The only person that could coach me through this is Shaunie, but she's not here to help me this time.

I muster all the strength I have and pull my body up slowly, turning off the water that has become ice cold. In an attempt to steady my breaths I think about something peaceful like the way I felt when Jun Pyo held me tonight as we danced. I haven't been held in ages and right now that thoughts seems to relax me.

I grab a towel hanging on a nearby rack and dry my body off and apply lotion to every part of me. Feeling a little calmer, I put the clothes on that Jun gave me while watching in the mirror how the t-shirt swallows my upper body.

Once back in the living room I see Jun sitting on the couch with similar pajamas as me but instead of sweatpants he has athletic shorts on. I take a seat opposite of him inhaling the small candle lit on the mantle. I can't seem to keep my eyes off the large portrait from earlier; it's the focal point of the living room.

"I hope your shower was okay, the water tends to get cold quickly in the guest room."

"It was fine, thank you." My eyes still haven't left the portrait and between my red puffy eyes and shaking voice I know how I feel is written all within my body language.

"I wanted to give you some news; I called Colonel Davis for an update about Dak."

My heart skips a beat and the shallow breaths I held in the bathroom try to escape as I slowly ask, "So what did he say?"

"He told me that Dak is in surgery right now but it looks like he'll be okay. That's all we have right now."

There's an intense pressure lifting from my heart hearing that Dak will be okay.

"I needed to hear that, I don't know what I'd do if he died from my own actions."

"Maverick, what do you mean? This wasn't your fault. I think you're being too hard on yourself."

"No I'm not. He was near me and I couldn't even see what he wanted. What if he had to tell me something important?" I stare at Jun sadly with tears streaming quietly down my face.

In an instant he closes the space between us on the couch and he sits next to me lightly rubbing my back to console me. The room is quiet as the candle continues flickering.

"I just don't know, it seems like there's something inside of me that's broken. I don't know how to describe it."

"Hey, can I share something with you?" he asks, looking into my eyes.

I nod my head yes.

"You see that picture hanging up? That is the first and last photo I have of my family all together. The woman holding me is my mother. She used to sing to me at night when I couldn't sleep. My father was a journalist and always knew how to tell a good story and knew how to have fun. And lastly you have my older sister Suni, she had one of the most infectious smiles that could make everyone else want to smile, too."

I look at Jun taking my eyes off the portrait. His eyes are glazed over and looking far away as he talks about his family.

"They sound like nice people. Where are they now?" I ask hesitantly, not sure why Jun keeps referring to them in the past tense.

"They are still in North Korea. Unfortunately, my father's job as a journalist cost our family. He published an article criticizing the government and became a political prisoner. It's kind of like a dream when I think about it. One day me and Suni were outside playing like we normally did after school. But instead of my father coming home by the time we were finished playing he didn't come. My mother got a call around dinner time that night and I just remember her face looking sad, the light in her eyes dying that day. My father was sent to prison and they wanted to do the same to my family, but instead of allowing that my mother did her best for me and Suni to leave. On the day we were set to leave my sister Suni said she couldn't leave mom by herself and instead of us both escaping that day only I did."

My heart aches for him and his family. I can do nothing but look at his face as his eyes continue to look at the portrait. "How old were you?"

"I was seven years old at the time and grew up in an orphanage once I made it to South Korea. I never tell this story to anyone but I'm telling you tonight because I want you to understand that even through all this I am still here. I know tonight was tough but none of this was your fault. In this type of job it's a risk we're all aware of that our lives could be in danger."

I shake my head, still reluctant to not blame myself. My head faces down with my chin almost in my chest.

"Listen. Hear me good. We are all meant to be in the place we need to be and tonight was just a part of that. I know it doesn't make sense right now, but we will find who was behind this attack. This isn't on you."

With his last sentence he places his hands underneath my chin lifting my face up. Our eyes meet and that quiet hungry energy fills the room, intoxicating my mind. Even with everything that's happened tonight I can't run away from the feelings that have been building up between us.

I said I wouldn't mix business with pleasure but for some reason I know the lines have already been blurred. I gulp loudly, steadying my eyes on Jun's lips.

Instead of waiting on logic to kick in I instinctively grab for him and smash my lips against his. The coldness in my body is replaced by heat and passion as I wrap my full lips around him. His tongue searches hungrily inside my mouth and his hands rest on the side of my waist. I want more and push his body back on the couch straddling his lap.

"Maverick, slow down I'm not sure this is the right decision right now. You've been through a lot tonight." He slowly pulls his face away from mine and stares intensely into my eyes. There's confusion written on his face like he's betraying himself.

"I know but something that I'm not confused about right now is you. I've been wanting to talk to you for a while about my feelings for you. But I thought you felt the same way, the way you protected me tonight and you always make me feel so safe. I thought I was reading your actions correctly."

My face is a mix of confusion and embarrassment. Feeling like I've made a fool of myself I remove my legs from around his waist and retreat to the couch pillow.

"I agree I've been protective over you but I was just doing my duties as your partner and I wanted to make you feel comfortable, like you belonged." The last word stumbles out of his mouth.

"Okay I get it. This was just a part of your job," I say, choking back tears and standing up quickly to run to the room. "Me coming to your house, you sharing that story, this was all bullshit."

I try my best not to look back and just walk quickly to the guest room. "I think it's better if I leave now."

"Maverick, hold on. Fuck, that's not what I meant."

I feel his strong arms grab my wrist to spin me around in the small hallway.

"Listen Maverick you aren't just some woman I met on the street. We work together but I can't help but want to protect you. The way you make me feel and what I have to do are two different things. And you didn't misunderstand my actions. What just happened between us was real, but it shouldn't... no it can't happen."

"Really," I say with one hand on my hip and the other still being held in place by his hand. I know he's right but I don't want to walk away empty handed. In some fucked up way I need a prize tonight to know at least one good thing happened.

Jun slowly opens his mouth again while I wait for him to keep telling me how wrong this would be, but no noise comes out. His mouth closes again forming a hard straight line.

He stares at me with his eyes burning into mine and within seconds he has me against the wall, his lips on mine again. I don't try to stop him because I want this and even though he may have second thoughts I know he wants me, too.

My lips part fully and Jun's hands start to roam my body feeling my ass and hips. I start to run my hands through his hair and moan softly as he pulls at the t-shirt I have on. I never thought he would be this forward because he's normally a gentleman but the way he lifts my shirt up feels animalistic. His hands roam under my shirt and he finds my breasts with no bra. There's easy access as my nipple slides between his fingers. All I can do is touch every part of him, his arms, chest, and neck.

"Maverick, if we do this there's no going back," he says coming up for air and looking me square in the eyes.

"That's a risk I'm willing to take," and with that I grab his face and kiss him like everything within me depends on it. My tongue seals our fate for the night as each kiss pulls me deeper into a feeling I never knew existed.

# Chapter 16

Ever since last night's escapade I can't do anything but think of this feeling I have that maybe what I did was right for a change. I could blame this feeling on the warm ache between my legs or the general want for more; either way I'm happy I stayed. Jun Pyo surprised me in more ways than one last night. Even though Dak's well-being rests on my mind, things seem lighter today. A genuine smile rests on my face as I see the sun rise sitting in a small inside garden space nestled in between the kitchen and living room.

"Good morning," Jun says walking up behind the chair I'm sitting in.

"Morning, I hope you don't mind. I grabbed some tea from your cabinets. I needed something to wake me up," I say sipping from the porcelain cup.

"Oh really. Well I could think of a few things to help with waking you up," he says seductively stepping in front of me.

"I think you showed me last night just how much you can keep me up," I say genuinely flashing back to the feeling between my legs remindings me of just how much I would love to go again.

"Well then prove it," he says boldly. His eyes travel down my body landing on my thick thighs as I sit in the chair with shorts on.

"You wish. You know you're way more playful than I thought you were, but really we have plenty of time for that stuff later," I say pointing to his toned abs as he stands shirtless.

"Oh really? What did you think of me when you first saw me?" he says pensively, taking a seat next to me.

I think for a minute of what to say, the first thought popping into my head was that I didn't know a Korean man could look that fine. But instead of mentioning that I said, "You were pretty intense and the way you kept staring at me during the first briefing. I just knew you would be hard to get along with."

Laughing lightheartedly he rubs his chin and touches his chest pretending to be hurt. "Wow, tell me how you really feel, Mav. I have to say when I first met you I didn't think we would connect like this." He straightens his posture, getting serious. "But there was something in your eyes that made me want to know you more. I'm not sure where this..." he points between us two "is going but I'm willing to see."

"Me too," I say admiring the way his face softens when he's comfortable. Reconsidering if a quickie is really something we can do later I bite my bottom lip. But just as soon as me and Jun's eyes connect I hear something. It's my phone.

"Excuse me." I pace to the guest bedroom in search of my phone. I grab it off the nightstand and look at the screen...

***Incoming Call: Shaunie***

I want to hold a grudge and let it go to voicemail but instead unlock my phone to answer.

"Hey Mav."

"Oh hello, Shaunie," I say, sounding unimpressed.

"Listen I know last time we spoke I said some hurtful things and you said some things. I wanted to say I'm sorry. I never should have mentioned the stuff about abortion. If you weren't ready I should have respected that."

I feel shocked. Shaunie never apologizes first. I can't speak for a few seconds. Even as kids I was always the one apologizing to make her feel better.

"Mav," she says my name when I don't respond. "This girl better not have hung up on me," Shaunie mutters.

"Yes Shaunie, I'm here. I appreciate your apology. That decision wasn't easy for me. It's a decision I live with every day, especially right now."

I tear up thinking about the follow up appointment about my fibroids. I hope Shaunie doesn't notice the change in my voice. Instead of focusing on my own problems I focus on an apology of my own.

"I'm sorry, too, Shaunie it wasn't right to bring up Jason. I knew it would hurt you that's why I said it."

"Me too," she says.

And just like that me and Shaunie fall into that familiar rhythm of normal. I catch Shaunie up on the gala and conveniently avoid mentioning Jun Pyo. She updates me on everything from crazy clients and how our mother keeps hinting at someone giving her grandkids.

After another thirty minutes of catching up I finally walk back into the kitchen. Taking a sip from the now cold tea, I pour the rest into the sink. The house seems unusually quiet with Jun Pyo gone. I set out to find him walking through the house admiring the soft blue paint on the walls and traditional photos hanging in the hallway.

As I get closer to Jun Pyo's room I hear his voice at a volume right above a whisper. The door is slightly cracked and my curiosity peaks as I lean my head in slightly.

"Yes that has been handled."

A few more moments of silence pass before I can hear anything else. I know I shouldn't be eavesdropping but my curiosity and intuition tell me otherwise.

"We are together now... He's stable but I'm not sure what he knows."

I assume he's talking to Colonel Davis which would explain why he hasn't been calling my phone. I hear Jun Pyo's feet moving under the wood panels indicating his conversation is over. I run quickly and just as I round the corner to the living room I stub my pinky toe. It takes all my strength not to yell out in pain. I proceed to hop on my right leg and stumble to the couch massaging my aching pinky toe.

Just as Jun Pyo walks in I place my phone in my hand pretending to look busy instead of looking guilty of snooping.

"I was just talking to my sister, we got into a fight about umm... something."

"Oh really? What were you arguing about?"

"Just sister stuff," I vaguely say not ready to share the real reason we were arguing.

"Well, that's a good reason to call."

I keep staring at my phone waiting for him to offer up details on his phone call but instead he's just as silent as I am. His demeanor even seems more tense and the warmth in his eyes from earlier is completely gone. I tread carefully on what I say next trying not to allude that I heard his conversation.

"Have you talked to Colonel Davis yet? I just know he's already lost his shit about the gala. I can picture him now with that vein in his forehead pulsing."

I'd tried my best to push the events from the Gala to the back of my mind because I was enjoying my time with Jun Pyo. But in no way was I mentally ready to discuss what happened without

feeling triggered. Jun Pyo looks at me weirdly with an expression I've never seen. Checking my mental rolodex I can't read him.

"Yes, I was speaking to him a few moments ago."

"So... what did he say about us–I mean about the gala and Dak?"

"He said that we'll need to see him first thing in the morning. Speaking of which, when would you like me to drop you off at home?"

"Damn, I didn't know you wanted me to leave," I say, sounding aggressive but really feeling hurt.

"Maverick, I don't mean it in that way, it's just that we can't let anyone in the office know what's going on and you also don't have anything here at my home. For the sake of us both it's best if you go home today."

"Wow, well I guess I'll start gathering my things."

Everything he said was true but it still doesn't help the sting in my chest. My phone in my hand starts ringing again. This time it's Dr. Zhong's office. Instead of avoiding the call I click to answer.

An automated voice comes on asking me to reschedule my ultrasound, but I hang up before I can make a selection. I can worry about that another day. I grab the purple blood-stained dress and shoes into my arms and stalk towards the door announcing to Jun Pyo that I'm ready to go home.

The gentleman he is opens the door for me and as he gets into the driver's side the last few hours seems to have vanished. I look at his neck with a hickey the size of Texas on it and I know what happened was no fantasy. But ever since that secretive call with Colonel Davis the mood has shifted. I want to ask him so badly what else did Colonel Davis mention; specifically if I would be fired but honestly I don't want to know.

***

Beep... Beep

I hear my phone alarm going off indicating it's time for my morning run. I wash my face and brush my teeth quickly ready to release my anxious energy with some physical activity. I catch the elevator to the main floor and within minutes of stretching, I take off like I'm in a track meet. I'm running like my life depends on it and can feel my heart speed up as people look in awe as I pass by.

It isn't until I check my Apple watch that I see I've run 3 miles in under thirty minutes. It's then that I stop running. After catching my breath I walk back towards my apartment.

This early in the morning the only people on the streets are older people and sanitation workers. I admire how clean the city is. From the subway to the streets everything seems so polished but one thing I can't get over is being looked at like a science experiment whenever a man looks me up and down not trying to hide his curiosity. I think about how normally this would piss me off, but I've learned I would be mad all the time if I focused on these things.

Selecting one final song to listen to until I get home I scroll my playlist looking for something that will ease my mind. After a few seconds I find the one; a song that can help me set the tone for my day. I press play on "Pick Up the Pieces" by Average White Band knowing that's exactly what I need to do today.

Once back at my apartment I shower and dress quickly so I can make it to the office on time. I sprint towards the subway station and get ready to learn the fate of my career and the repercussions of the gala.

After thirty minutes I'm finally in the office and walk past multiple agents giving me the most pitiful faces I've ever seen. They must be thinking about how troubled I look with the blood and expressionless face from the gala all tattooed in their brains. Instead of reliving that moment I try my best to smile in the midst of this mess that equals my first career fail.

I wave hello to our receptionist but before I can turn left towards my office she tells me Colonel Davis wants to see me now and that Jun Pyo is also waiting. The butterflies in my stomach start to dance with each step I take closer to Colonel Davis' office. I knock first and turn the knob gently, seeing Colonel Davis and Jun Pyo sitting down already.

"Maverick, please sit down, let's not waste any time I need a full debrief on what occurred don't leave anything out."

I proceed to tell Colonel Davis almost all the events of the night except my conversation with Darcelle. As I describe the events of the evening I relive the shock and surprise of Dak being shot and the drones firing throughout the gala event.

Colonel Davis stares at me like I've grown a second head once I finish recounting my version of what happened.

"So, nothing else occurred, Lieutenant?"

"No, that was it."

"Well, I would say this is something else," he says throwing down a large file with me and Darcelle pictured together. My jaw hits the floor and my eyes travel back and forth between Jun Pyo and Colonel Davis.

"Where did you get this from?"

"The where is not as important as the *why*. Explain why you would be talking to an assumed terrorist that plotted with former leadership to destroy this department."

"Listen, I just thought she could provide us with more information about Violetta Stone, but she didn't tell me anything. I didn't want to spook her so I didn't formally alert anyone except Jun Pyo and Agent Choy."

"That much is certain. You're lucky she decided to share this information otherwise we would be having a very different conversation."

"But I don't understand I was just talking to her, sir."

"You don't talk to her. This makes this operation look bad. What if the media got ahold of this? Do you know how this looks? We don't need anymore of our leadership getting wrapped up in gossip or a conspiracy theory. Our relationship here is very fragile between the American government and South Korea."

"I didn't realize talking to her was such an issue. It hasn't even been proven yet that her associate Violetta was even the real mole." My nostrils start to flare with how the Colonel is talking to me.

"And just what exactly do you mean by that statement, Robinson?" His vein starts to flare up letting me know he's angry with his skin turning light pink.

It feels like Jun Pyo is just a fly on the wall as me and Colonel Davis have a tennis match with our eyes.

"Let's just all remain calm, Colonel Davis, Mav—-I mean Lieutenant Robinson did alert me but we thought it was an opportunity to possibly get more information from Darcelle that could help us," says Jun Pyo.

As usual he tries to save the day and it almost makes my brain forget I want to be mad at him.

"I don't care what you two thought you were doing. We have dead bodies and an agent in a coma, and now the one possible connection we have is in the wind. And can either of you even explain why Dak was even there?"

"I'm not sure," I say silently, with a half-truth avoiding mentioning Dak wanting to tell me something.

"We are not certain of the reason why that agent was there but I can promise you we will get to the bottom of who is responsible" Jun Pyo says quickly working to diffuse the situation.

" That's not good enough. You two lead this operation and it seems like you have no clue on what went wrong. This has cost us important leaders not to mention even more pressure from the States to have someone in custody."

"But sir, this wasn't our fault," I try to defend us but Colonel Davis waves his hand dismissively in the air.

My mouth forms a hard line and nothing else is said for a few seconds.

"I understand this was your first time leading this type of assignment Lieutenant Robinson and Jun but this mistake has cost us. Now normally I would be ready to look for replacements for both of you. But this time it will only be a warning, but as for you Miss Robinson you are suspended for a week. Agent Jun you will coordinate with Agent Choy while Robinson is out, is that clear?"

"Yes sir," we both say unenthusiastically.

"Colonel Davis, if I may ask. Why am I suspended?"

The vein in his forehead pulses again and everything within him strains at me with such intensity.

"Miss Robinson you're already treading on thin ice, but to be completely blunt you allowed Darcelle Ramirez to infiltrate this event and didn't take precautions even with her history with this department. You're lucky I don't do more than suspend you."

"I understand Colonel Davis, and I promise nothing like this will ever happen again."

"I would hope so. Now you're both dismissed."

As I get up slowly deflated from failing my first mission and a suspension, I can't help but feel uneasy. Me and Jun Pyo exit the office. Even though the conversation is over my nostrils are still flared from the adrenaline and anger pumping through my veins.

I tread back to my office passing by Agent Choy's empty desk thinking what gave her the right to share that information with Colonel Davis. She tried to make me look bad I think to myself, even after all the fake acceptance I guess you never really know people's intentions.

I firmly hold my fists in tight knuckles ready to punch something and as I enter my office and turn around abruptly I realize Jun Pyo has been walking with me. The look on his face is that of a sad puppy. I can tell he feels sorry for me just in the way he closes my office door and gently walks towards my desk I'm leaning against.

"Mav, I'm sorry about the suspension. I didn't think he would react this harshly."

"Neither did I–I just can't understand why Choy would mention Darcelle to him. As far as we know this is an unrelated attack. Not to mention he was so quick to want to get rid of me, like I don't deserve a fair chance to prove myself. I don't know, maybe it's a black thing or woman thing…"

I stop mid-sentence not really sure if I want to have this conversation. I'm not really sure how to explain these types of things to someone that isn't black. I hope Jun Pyo doesn't question what I mean, but the confused look on his face tells it all.

"What do you mean by that? I don't think he was intentionally being cruel to you."

"I don't mean that it's just maybe he's not allowing me the same amount of chances as everyone else." I try to skirt around what I really want to say before I have another reason to be angry.

"Well Mav, as a leader it's expected that we are put under a microscope when we make mistakes. It's not just us that we have to worry about, it's everyone. But mistakes happen in this type of field. I just wish we could've avoided this one."

"Look, I'm going to be honest. I don't know if you could ever understand how it feels to be me. As a black woman here, as a woman in leadership, there is a lot of pressure for me to get things right the first time. And if I do make a mistake it's something that will follow me for the rest of my career. If you haven't noticed there aren't too many women that look like me in this type of position."

"I understand Mav, truly I do." His voice softens and he grabs my hands pulling me closer to him. I rest my head on his shoulder and inhale his scent and just like that I can feel my body release the tension from a few minutes ago.

He whispers in my ear how everything is going to be alright and assures me with kisses to my temple. I get lost in his arms as we stand there embracing in my office. After a few more minutes we pull away from each other.

"Are you sure you're okay?"

"Yes," I say, scrounging up a smile for him.

"Alright. Well then I'm going to see you later, don't be too hard on yourself."

"Okay."

As he gives me one last look before leaving his office I see that fire burning behind his eyes again. I wish he could do more than assure me with words right now, I want him to assure me with something else.

As my mind starts to twist into scenes of the two of us against my wooden desk I hear a quick knock thinking it's Jun Pyo. I quickly say, "Back already?"

But instead it's the receptionist.

"Lieutenant Maverick, do you have a few minutes?"

"Sure, what can I do for you?"

"According to these records we're still missing your official physical... "She starts shuffling through some papers and continues. "It says here we're missing details from your Obstetrician. We were waiting for her results from a recent visit."

"I'm sorry, I've been meaning to follow up with them. I'll schedule an appointment immediately." She thanks me and quietly exits. I was lying through my teeth. I've been putting off the ultrasound, but no more waiting. It's time I stop running and know what's really going on.

# Chapter 17

It's day three of my week-long suspension and it seems like all I've been able to do is feel sorry for myself. I've barely bathed or left the house, and have been skipping my morning runs. But today I'm going to get my ultrasound so it's time I finally crawl out of my shell.

I stare blankly at my TV screen rewatching episodes of "Boys Over Flowers" tapping my phone quickly. I see it's almost time for the appointment and pause my show. I have just enough time to shower and create something out of the nest on top of my head.

Once I make it to the doctor's office, my stomach is doing full somersaults. My need to avoid makes me wish I could run out of this office. I glance at the door as a pregnant woman waddles in and just as I think about taking the opportunity to leave my name is called. I walk back to the private room and undress shortly after so I can get prepped for the ultrasound.

I hear a light tap as someone asks if I'm finished undressing. I say yes and Dr. Zhong enters the room looking cheerful.

She says, "Miss Robinson, what a pleasure for you to come back. I thought for sure you had forgotten about the ultrasound."

"No Doctor, I have just been really busy with work but I'm here now," I say wanting to move things along.

She stares at me like she doesn't believe me but all that comes out of her mouth is, "Then I assume we are both ready now. Please lie back on the bed."

The exam lasts for at least an hour which I find a little unusual per my nerves. According to Google this exam should only take twenty minutes max.

It starts with a cold gel being rubbed on my stomach and the ultrasound machine being placed there shortly after. I thought that would be the end of it, but Dr. Zhong uses another ultrasound machine that has to be placed inside my vagina.

The entire time the room is quiet and all I hear is the medical machine and my heartbeat pumping through my ears. Once the whole ordeal is done I sit up and look at Dr. Zhong expecting bad news.

"Miss Robinson—"

"Please, Call me Maverick. I think we've moved beyond a last name basis, Doctor," I try to offer in humor to replace my nervousness.

"Okay Maverick, I would like to discuss what I've seen today from the exam."

"Okay," I say, holding my breath until she says something else."

"Your exam is a little concerning. I do see a few very small fibroids along your uterine wall which may require surgical removal, but I don't think it should be too difficult for them to stay if you decide not to have surgery."

"And what if I want to have children? I'm not planning to right now but maybe in the future."

"Children are still very much possible for you. Most of the time the presence of fibroids doesn't mean you can't have kids. However, it can mean complications or even pregnancy loss. Again this doesn't always happen. For a woman of your ummm… ethnicity, it's, unfortunately, a higher risk. I assure you that whatever happens, I am able to help you."

Thank you, Doctor Zhong, but what do you mean someone of my ethnicity has higher chances of fibroids, isn't this something all women have to worry about?"

"Yes, it affects all women, but as an African American woman your chances are higher."

"And what if I get surgery? Would that get rid of this completely?"

"If you decide to get surgery it can remove the small tumors already present but it doesn't prevent additional growth. I know this may be hard to digest so let's schedule a follow-up where you have some time to think about if surgery is right for you."

"I think that's a good idea."

"Okay, until next time Maverick."

She gives me a small pat on the hand before she exits, leaving me with my thoughts.

Once I leave the doctor's office I figure since I'm already out and I have absolutely nothing to do at home I'll visit Dak in the hospital. Jun Pyo found out which hospital he was at and told me he could use a friend.

I catch a train not far from Dr. Zhong's office and find myself standing outside room 32. I debate knocking but remember the nurse saying Dak has been unconscious since his arrival. I walk in quietly ready to leave when I look at Dak; his body full of tubes and monitors beeping. He looks unrecognizable but somewhere underneath is the first real friend I met when I got here. A few tears well up in my eyes but it's soon replaced by anger as I think about how the attack from the gala caused a mess that has thrown my life into disarray.

"I promise Dak, I will make this right if it's the last thing I do." I kiss his left hand gently and leave the hospital ready to finally get the truth about this mole, this attack, and whatever else is being hidden.

The depression hovering over me seems to disappear with this newfound motivation to get to the bottom of the truth. Once I get home I'll do my research into this mole. I've been so focused on Violetta that I didn't see anyone else in the picture.

I feel renewed as I decide to take the thirty-minute walk to my house instead of the train. I let out a hard breath as my phone buzzes in my hand.

My mother is calling. Instead of pressing decline like I normally do, I answer and listen to her talk for a few minutes.

"Hey my Mavvy it's Mom, I just wanted to check on you."

"Thanks Mom, I appreciate you calling," I say genuinely.

I want to tell her what's been going on. Maybe she can help me or knows what it's like to be experiencing the things I'm going through. I think I can be vulnerable again with my mom and I am ready to tell her the truth about what's been occurring over the last few months.

"Mavvy, you know I've been thinking. Are there any good men over there? I mean ones that look like you. God forbid you find a good-looking man over there that's not black you know I always wanted you girls to have children that look like our family."

The line grows quiet.

"Mavvy, are you still there?" Mom asks.

I can't let her dictate this conversation anymore and finally give her a piece of my mind so that I can finally have peace from the expectations she forces on me.

"Listen, Mom, I'm about to say something to you as respectfully as I can. I love you but you're tripping, putting all this pressure on me. Do you know that I'm the only black woman in leadership at my job? Did you also know that I've been to multiple states and countries? Huh…none of that was the result of a man or a baby. I want children, God knows I do but it's not going to happen just because you keep talking to me about it. I love you but please stop making me feel bad or not good enough just because my life isn't like yours. And by the way you would have a grandchild if you weren't so damn selfish".

This time it's my mother who is silent. Before she can respond I tell her I'll call her back later once I'm free. The freedom I feel right now is unmatched, my mother finally knows how I feel. I just hope she listens and stops pressuring me and that comment about having brown babies was insensitive. I can't believe she would say something like that.

My phone rings again and I'm tempted to just turn my phone off but I look at the screen and see it's Jun Pyo calling. My mood shifts. I don't know whether to be happy because he's calling or upset because

I haven't heard from him since he came to my office. Feeling conflicted, I answer the phone anyway.

"What a surprise, Jun Pyo I wasn't expecting to hear from you," I say formally like he's just a coworker and not the man that had me screaming out his name a few days ago at his house.

"I've been a little busy since you've been out, but I was calling to see if you would like to have dinner with me tonight?"

"Tonight?"

"I know it's short notice, but I need to see you."

"Okay, let's meet at the outdoor food market on Gangnam Street. I'm craving those dumpling things. What do you call them?"

"You mean mandu, but I thought you didn't like street food," he says, laughing at me.

"Well it's better than the restaurants, but let's meet there at seven."

"Okay then it's a date, I'll see you later."

"You will," and with that, we both hang up. I look at my phone like a schoolgirl smiling thinking about those dumplings and Jun Pyo. I can't wait until 7:00.

It doesn't take long for me to get back to my place but before I enter the building I decide to indulge in some self-care. I walk further down the street and stop in front of the bathhouse sauna and spa. I've only seen depictions of a bathhouse on television. If it's accurate I anticipate a whole bunch of old women gossiping and soaking in a large tub scrubbing each other's back. I walk in hesitant and unsure of what to do next.

The bath house is much more than I expected and instantly I know I made the right choice. There's soft relaxing music playing in the background and cherry blossoms sprayed across the front entrance along with a small cascading waterfall. I walk towards a large dark oak desk and see a middle-aged Korean woman behind the counter. We both stare at each other, looking as confused as I'm about to be.

In broken Korean I say, " Could you help me? I want to get spa services."

She still looks confused and just when I think my intro to speaking Korean class has failed me a younger woman walks towards me and has the same look on her face as the first woman.

Instead of only staring, she asks in English, "How can I help you?"

I explain that I want a massage, sauna, and bathhouse experience. I'm instructed to change into a robe and take my clothes off in an area with large lockers.

The bathhouse is the first part of my experience and when I see the inside of a large-looking cave and steam warming an Olympic-sized pool takes my breath away. I've never seen anything like this in the States but it's amazing and surprisingly it's almost empty. There are a few women in a corner talking when suddenly they stop at the sight of me. I don't let it bother me as I take off my robe and place it on a nearby lounge chair. I stick my toes into the water and find it's the perfect temperature, submerging my body.

I find myself relaxing the afternoon away after massages, and after a sauna visit, I feel at total peace. Once my clothes are back on I head to the front desk leaving a hefty tip which earns me a wide smile from the Korean lady behind the desk. I look at my phone and see it's about 5:00; just enough time for me to get ready for my date.

***

"Can I please have another order of mandu, please?" I say smiling at Jun Pyo as I place my second order of dumplings for the night.

"So how was your day at the office?" I ask.

"Nothing too interesting, there will be some changes once you get back."

"Changes like what?" I choke out my words worried about my future.

"Nothing too alarming. You and Agent Choy will be..." he pauses. "Kind of partnering together to run the department for a while. Just as you continue to get comfortable with the way things are done there."

My blood boils and any relaxation held from earlier completely dissipates with this news of having a partner.

"What do they mean partnership? I can handle myself without someone else's help. This is Colonel Davis' way of kicking me out like they did Violetta Stone." I say a little too quickly before I can stop myself.

Jun Pyo looks like I just said Voldermort's name in a scene from a Harry Potter movie and I could swear his face goes pale, but what comes out of his mouth is the opposite. All he says is, "I don't think he's doing that. He mentioned because she knew imperative information that couldn't be shared yet that her partnership would be important towards our next operation."

"Order of mandu up," an older Korean man yells even though we're sitting right in front of his food cart. I grab the order quickly and stuff my mouth until I'm ready to say more.

"I don't know what's more surprising; that he's ready to replace me so quickly or Agent Choy would even take this opportunity behind my back without even talking to me first as her superior. Honestly, I would be less shocked if they allowed Eun Ji to partner with me. Even though I can't stand her or the way she looks at you I would've seen it coming."

Jun Pyo takes my hands which are covered in dumpling grease and kisses my cheek. The older man that just handed me my food gives him a thumbs up.

"What was that for?"

"Did I ever tell you it's cute when you act jealous? You have nothing to worry about. Eun Ji doesn't stand a chance against you." He looks at me in a way that can't be explained but I know what it means.

"Umm check please," I say ready to leave.

Jun Pyo laughs "Slow down, I had something else special planned for us'.

"What could be better than having you inside of me?" I whisper into his ear.

I move my body backwards hoping to have caught Jun Pyo off guard and just like I knew he would his cheeks seem warm, and he smiles. He clears his throat; a habit I've noticed happens when he's flustered.

He tells me the last part of our date is supposed to be a visit to the Namsan Tower for a romantic view of the whole city. The tower is within walking distance of the street market, so we opt to walk instead of take his car. The way the tower points into the sky it seems massive, as an array of led lights move to music playing throughout the square. Straight ahead of us the tower stands and small dessert shops lay to the left and right of the tower.

As we walk closer to the tower, I see tourists taking pictures with the tower in the background just as we near the entrance to the observation deck, I see a short woman selling roses nearby. My eyes linger a little longer than usual and Jun Pyo catches me staring. In an instant he's at the lady's side handing her a few bills and she hands him all the roses in her hand, fifteen to be exact.

"I thought you would like these," he says walking back over to me with the roses in hand.

"Thank you, that was very sweet of you."

Caught off guard from his sweet gesture, I have the roses in one hand and use the other to walk hand in hand with him. The woman that he brought the flowers from just looks on either in shock or awe. I can't quite tell.

After Jun Pyo pays for our tickets to go to the observation deck, I'm in awe of the view. You can see everything this high up. The chill from the night air feels stronger at this height and my legs tremble since I have on a skirt. He sees me trembling and offers his jacket to me. I take it and we both stand there quietly.

It isn't until a few minutes have passed that we continue talking. It always surprises me how easy he is to talk to. We stay there until we are the only people left. It wasn't long before the attendant tells us the tower is closing. We both look surprised as the attendant starts ushering us toward the elevator back down the tower.

I'm just as excited to get back to my apartment and quench this fire burning inside of me. The walk to his car seems endless and even longer a drive to my apartment, which is only ten minutes away.

Jun Pyo follows me upstairs after parking his car. Once inside the apartment I waste no time clawing at his neck and kissing him. He kisses me back hard trying to match my movements. It feels like I can barely breathe but I love this feeling. In an instant the kisses stop and Jun Pyo stares at me in the moonlight of my apartment I can see his face contorting again.

"Don't think just act," I say, wanting to keep him here with me in the present instead of the far away place his mind wants to take him.

"I'm just trying to remember your face; you're just so beautiful." He cups my face with his hands and we continue kissing. The quick lusty kisses have stopped and now they seem more intense. He takes his time massaging the back of my head. I don't know what comes over me but in between the touching and feeling I have a moment of word vomit that really should have been a private thought.

"I think I'm falling for you," I say with my eyes wide and pleading for him to say the same but instead all I get is a kiss that leaves me confused.

My body wants to keep going but my heart tells me this feels all too familiar. The type of story that plays out with me falling too soon and not getting that energy back. But my heart can wait. My body will lead the way tonight and because of this I fall into the decision that has always worked for a girl like me.

"I'm ready," I tell Jun Pyo, leading him over to my couch.

He points towards the stairs towards my bedroom, but I shake my head leading the way. Our clothes are off in an instant and Jun Pyo reaches in his pants pocket for something. After a few moments he looks at me with his hands empty.

"I don't have any condoms... would you happen to have any?"

"No, but we can still have sex. I mean it's not like I can get pregnant right now."

"I don't really know if that's a good idea. I've never really had sex without condoms… what about risks?"

I can tell just by how wide his eyes grow he's embarrassed, confused, but most of all conflicted with doing this. I know if we keep talking, we won't have sex. I approach him closer with the hunger of a lion approaching a gazelle. I can hear him still talking but play deaf to his pleas as I nibble on his neck, ears, and shoulder. Once I get to just the right spot, he's not talking anymore. I straddle his lap and whisper in his ear.

"We'll be safe," I say and do the unthinkable sliding right on top of him without permission. His eyes grow wide, and he can't contain himself. The beast I know to be lurking beneath those eyes made of stone comes to life as I grind slowly against him. I know I've gone too far but the truth is I was already gone.

# Chapter 18

This morning feels kind of like a dream as I hear light snoring from the left side of my bed and see Jun Pyo's bare chest on my comforter. I'm not sure what has taken over, but my actions last night felt good in the moment. After waking up, though, I feel the guilt in me rising. I got what I wanted but at what cost? I was selfish and ended up doing exactly what I said I wouldn't do. I turn my body opposite of Jun Pyo with my back to him silently pleading with my heart about my body's carnal desires.

My mind is so wrapped up I don't hear my phone ringing until it's went to voicemail.

***Missed Call from Shaunie***

I decide to call her back later but instead my phone rings again with her name appearing. I answer the phone above a whisper, so I don't wake Jun Pyo.

"Hey Shaunie."

"Hey sis… why are you whispering like you got a man over there or something? I know you're usually up by now with your morning run."

I clear my throat, not sure if I should tell her she's right I decide to spill the beans I've already done enough lying.

"Actually, I do have a man here, but why you are calling me so early Shaunie?"

"Damn Mav! Tell me it was that sexy ass British driver! Girl, I would kill for an Idris Elba-type to take me right here right now. All he would have to say is one sentence with that accent and it's done I'm getting folded like a pretzel."

"No, it wasn't him," I say second-guessing sharing with her.

I roll over to see if Jun Pyo is still sleeping but don't take any risk and go downstairs to the living room to continue my conversation. I share the details I know will peak Shaunie's interest like how we met technically at a store and how he makes me feel. I also share with her the weight I've been carrying about having fibroids and possibly risk never having children.

We both cry a little and she tells me how she doesn't think there's someone out there that's her soulmate because otherwise he would've found her already. Even though we are thousands of miles apart I connect with my sister like she's right next to me in this moment we are both vulnerable.

My heart skips a beat as I look up and see Jun Pyo walking down the stairs headed towards the kitchen. Due to the lack of walls in this place I hope he didn't hear all my conversation. There are some parts of my life I can't share yet with him, including what I've done in the past.

Before I can acknowledge him, his phone suddenly vibrates on the couch. He looks worried taking his call in the bathroom. I wrap up my conversation with Shaunie after a few more minutes of talking before lightly tapping on the bathroom door.

"Hey, is everything okay in there?" I ask.

"Yes," he says quickly, but I don't believe him and find myself snooping on him. I can't hear much with the door mostly closed but I hear a sliver of conversation.

Jun Pyo mentions how someone doesn't know something, he repeats this statement multiple times. I'm not sure if he's talking about me in particular but the next few words, I hear get rid of any doubt. I push my ear closer to the door and overhear more.

"She's innocent in all this... no, she doesn't know why Dak wanted to talk to her; he's still unconscious."

My mind starts racing and I'm tempted to open the door fully just to figure out who he's talking to. Before I can decide if I want to keep listening I hear Jun Pyo preparing to end the call

"Listen, whatever you do I don't want Maverick to get caught up in this. You guys can't repeat the same mistake. She is not Violetta. Don't contact me, I'll call you... *annyeong.*" He says above a whisper saying bye in Korean.

I think silently to myself. *What I should do?* On one hand I feel betrayed about what I've heard but also confused. What does Violetta have to do with anything? Not wanting my face to betray what I've heard I put on the best poker face I can summon as Jun Pyo exits the bathroom.

He kisses me on the forehead softly plopping on the sofa. I silently debate with myself about addressing what I heard or continue acting clueless.

"Are you okay Maverick? You look sick." He rushes over examining my face and touching my cheek.

"I'm fine," I do my best to remove his hand from my cheek, gritting my teeth trying to hold my composure.

"We need to talk about last night. I told you I wasn't sure about what happened and you... you just did what you wanted. Maybe this is an American thing but in my culture it's not something done freely unless we are married," Jun Pyo says.

"But you didn't stop me. I don't remember you pushing me off or putting up a fight."

My words come out like a fist landing a punch on the defense. "Besides it won't happen ever again. I can promise you that."

"Don't try to flip this on me, Maverick, this is serious. You know how I feel about you but..."

I interrupt quickly "No, I don't know how you feel about me that's the damn problem."

His face looks hurt, but his words are an arsenal ready to attack me. "You don't know but *you* were ready to fuck me. I knew your type of women were different when it came to sleeping with men..."

What do you mean 'your type of woman'? What the hell is that supposed to mean? If you're saying what I think you are I promise you will see what my kind of people are capable of." My voice starts elevating as I wait for him to answer.

"That's not what I meant... I mean an American woman. You always think the world is out to get you just because you're a black woman."

"I knew this wouldn't work. Was this some type of challenge to you? Did you just want to live out some fantasy through me, Jun Pyo? Do I really mean that little to you that you would generalize me with other women? I would think you of all people would know the difference."

"You still don't understand. I just mean that you're different sexually than the women I'm used to. Last night you made me feel like no one before you counts. I've never been with any woman that intimately. If I'm being completely honest, I just want more... more of this," he says gently.

My body's natural response to cave into his plea disappears at the thought of knowing he's hiding a secret.

"Maverick, are you still here? Come on," he says waving his hand in front of my face. "I'm sorry I overreacted. You just make me feel... like confused about things."

"What exactly is confusing, Jun Pyo? I've told you how I feel multiple times and you always pull back from me like you're hiding something. Is this a game to you?"

My words hang in the air while I wait for a genuine answer. His face contorts like he wants to tell me something, but he doesn't and all we can do is stare at each other.

"I... I've felt confused because I wasn't expecting this," he pauses and I hang onto his words waiting. "I wasn't expecting this to feel so much like the real thing," he says more to himself than me.

"Why wouldn't it feel real to you?" I say with my eyebrows scrunched in confusion.

His eyes plead with me not to ask further questions.

"I'll talk to you later, Maverick."

He walks towards the couch again grabbing his belongings quickly. As he walks past me and tries to give me a gentle kiss on the forehead but I move just of his reach and he's left with a stunned expression. One last look at me and he's out the door.

I'm left second-guessing myself as I figure out if I've been betrayed yet again by someone I trusted. It seems like every man I allow into my heart lies to me. I sit down on the couch tapping my foot anxiously. I bend down slightly off the couch to pick up an accent pillow.

As I place it back on the couch I notice a phone on the floor, but it's not mine. It must have slipped out of Jun Pyo's pants pocket or something. The phone fits easily in my hand and I flip it over analyzing it. Yeah, this must be Jun Pyo's phone but it doesn't look like the one he normally carries.

I trace my finger over the phone icon and see it's a prepaid phone; the type you use when you don't want to be monitored or tracked. After touching the phone screen I see a generic background photo of the ocean and a lock screen stopping me from unlocking the device. This is my chance to get the answers I need.

After walking upstairs in search of my work laptop I scramble to decrypt the phone. I plug in a small cord that connects the phone to my laptop and I pace silently waiting.

Before I can even go to the decryption screen I hear knocking on my door that's persistent and leaves me staring. I grab the phone and put it in my bra so it's hidden. Looking through the peephole, I see it's Jun Pyo back again probably looking for his phone.

I scream through the door not sure if letting him in is a good idea "What do you want?"

"Could I please come in? I think I left my wallet."

"No, it's not here." I state quickly hoping he'll go away.

"Please it would make me feel more comfortable if I could come in and check myself."

"Fine, but hurry up," I say before unlocking the door and adjusting the phone in my bra so it can't be seen.

He walks past me and straight to the couch moving pillows, cushions, and sliding the couch forward looking for his "wallet." I know he's really looking for the phone. By now he's on all fours looking on the floor and under things and checking the same spots he's looked at before. After endless minutes of searching, he still can't locate what he's looking for.

"It's time for you to go. I don't think your ph…I mean wallet is here," I say almost spilling the beans knowing what he's really looking for.

"I think you're right. Maybe I just left it in my car."

"Okay, well you can leave now. Bye," I say getting straight to the point.

He looks at me the way he does when he wants to touch me, feel me, and kiss me but instead he says goodbye like it's the last time he'll ever say it again. And for once there's nothing else, I want to do to get him to stay.

After he leaves, I lock the top and bottom lock for extra security, not sure if he'll try to come back. My heart pulses with confusion prepared for the worst.

I grab my work laptop and the cell phone ready to find out the truth. The decryption is just about done and with each second that passes I can't tell if I should be happy or heartbroken.

Finally, after fifteen minutes I'm in. The first place I go is to recent text messages. Only one thread exists from an unknown number. Some of the messages are in Korean but there are a few in English. The one that catches my attention first:

*Unknown: Have you slept with her yet?*

*J: Yes*

I continue scrolling as a horrible feeling starts to bubble in my stomach.

*Unknown: V. Stone problem, can you take action*

*J:Action Taken*

The first message at the very top of the thread causes my heart to all but implode.

*Unknown: She's arriving today from Houston. Make sure you get close with her we can't take any chances*

I throw the phone on the floor hard enough that the screen is cracked, and glass shards lay at my feet. He's been playing me from the very beginning.

# Chapter 19

"Now paging Doctor Zhen for a code blue."

A speaker over my head squeaks out the instruction as I stand outside Dak's room. I can hear movement inside, but mentally I'm not sure if I should even be here, I am still having trouble facing the fact that Dak got shot because of me but my chance to escape becomes fleeting as a nurse walks by.

"You can go in at any time miss, the patient is doing well enough for visitors today."

I smile gently and take this as my sign to find the courage to open the door. Putting on my bravest face and voice. Not knowing what to say or expect I enter the room surprised to see Dak's backside as he hobbles towards his bed.

"I love the nightgown look on you, especially the back."

In traditional Dak fashion, he spins around and smiles at me the same way he did when I first met him. In his deep surly voice with the British accent at an all-time high all he can say is, "Now you can say you've seen me almost naked *innit.*"

"I guess I can. What are you doing out of bed anyway? Shouldn't you be resting or for God's sake laying down?"

"Well ,excuse me Mum but I will. Give me a break. I'm healing but that doesn't mean I'm confined to the bed besides I still have to use the loo."

"It's clear your injuries haven't affected your sense of humor. But get serious with me for a moment. Dak, I thought you were going to die. I can't even lie it's a miracle to be sitting here talking with you… there was so much blood that night." My eyes become cloudy with tears wanting to escape but I keep them at bay by looking out the window.

"Shit, I didn't think I would either… I mean one moment I'm trying to tell you something and the next I just hear shots ringing out. Everything was a blur *innit*, I just wish I could've managed to avoid getting shot… What happened anyway? Did you find out who was behind that attack?"

"Let's just say your guess is as good as mine. I'm out of the loop and currently not sure when I'll be back seeing as how I'm on suspension and managed to get demoted." The words spill out of my mouth hurriedly with contempt.

"Woah, what do you mean you got suspended?"

For the next hour and a half, I explain to Dak just how much things have changed since the shooting. The details of me being played by Jun Pyo and finding out he is a snake is something I'm not ready to share yet, so I leave that part out of my story. I can't help but stare at Dak and see how thin he has gotten. Laying on the bed his face is the same but I can tell that his body will take more time to get back to normal.

"Maverick, I realize before all the commotion I didn't get a chance to tell you something; something important. But before I tell you I just need to know that you're not going to lose your shit."

"Dak, if it's about me being the reason you were shot at the gala, I already feel terrible about it. I mean I didn't know what to think when I saw you there with Darcelle of all people. I just thought—"

"Maverick, take it down a wee bit, love. I wasn't talking about that. What do you mean it's your fault? The only person responsible for that shooting was the person controlling the drones. There was no way you knew that would happen."

"Dak, you don't know how much pressure that takes off me.. I've been feeling guilty ever since that night. I just couldn't shake seeing you lying there helpless," I shake my head in distress. "I couldn't forgive myself if you had…" I can't complete my sentence.

"Maverick, this isn't on you," he says trying to get out of bed again.

I quickly stand up from the chair near his bedside and stop him. With one hand on the bed railing and the other on Dak's shoulder, I push his body back down.

"Thank you Dak, but you know you're still supposed to be in this bed healing," I say smiling widely. "Here, let me get your pillow," I pat it gently leaning forward so that I'm hovering just over Dak's face.

Not sure if the tensions are high because I thought he would die but Dak reaches for my waist to pull me near for a tight hug. My body melts against his and for a second my heart feels light but just as soon as I pull away, I feel the heavy tug of Jun Pyo weighing me down.

"Thank you for coming to visit me Maverick. Truly it means a lot."

"You're welcome … now what did you want to tell me?"

I sit back down in my seat and listen intently for the next ten minutes as Dak goes into detail to talk about Darcelle and how they both believe in Violetta's innocence. But what he says last has me feeling lost.

What Dak proceeds to tell me leaves my heart sinking even further. Not only is Violetta innocent but she was set up. I hold my breath with every sentence being repeated. I'm not sure if he knows that the person who set up Violetta was Jun Pyo. For some reason I can't even tell him what I know. I shouldn't protect Jun Pyo, but I don't have the heart to say anything.

"Look, I know you thought I was being overly cautious when I told you to be careful. Darcelle has reason to believe Agent Jun Pyo set Violetta up."

"What do you mean by that? Do you have proof?"

'Not yet, but we will." Dak says his soft handsome features turning hard.

"Well, whatever the plan is I'm in."

"I don't know Maverick, this is dangerous. We really don't know who we're going up against."

"I don't care. This is personal," I state confidently, stating my truth.

***

Over the next few days, me and Dak's plan to expose Jun Pyo swings into motion. The first thing I do is work on gathering proof to expose him to Colonel Davis. Unfortunately, finding proof won't be easy. This is my last day off before my suspension ends and I have to go back to the office tomorrow. I need to find something; anything that can give us a chance to reveal the truth.

After combing through case files, I locate Jun Pyo's file before he started working in the military. It turns out he did tell the truth about his family, but instead of being raised in an orphanage he basically was a ghost from the age of seven to eighteen. Apparently, this is common in Seoul, especially during the time a lot of family's children were fleeing from North Korea. *This is just another lie I can add to what he's told me.*

My next step is to investigate assignments Violetta partnered with Jun Pyo on. Dak tells me this is the key to finding what we need. With my access I can see most of her files easily and read each log of events thoroughly. After reading dozens of cases I see a pattern. All her cases either ended up botched or the asset she's protecting goes missing or worse, ends up dead. There is no way these cases could have all ended like this; even simple surveillance results in a failed mission.

As I continue reviewing the notes, I see Jun Pyo's signature next to statements. The assignment usually goes left as soon as Violetta takes over her part of the mission. This is a good pattern but it's not enough for me to bring it up to Colonel Davis. Instead of appealing to Violetta's innocence all this does is make her look worse.

Frustrated and empty-handed, I step away from my laptop ready to throw it against the wall. Recalling the moments I spent with Jun Pyo, I try to think of something real he told me that could help me prove his real agenda. The story about his dad must be something that can help me figure out who he's connected to.

Opening my laptop again, I search for family connection in Jun Pyo's file... it's empty. I think back to the story he told me about his family. What was his sister's name? I type in *Sung Jun* with the search criteria in North Korea family member of political prisoner. No results.

"Wait, her name was Suni, "I say out loud.

I type in the same details and find Suni Jun, her file doesn't mention anything about having a brother but what I do find is a lengthy rap sheet. Apparently Suni was associated with a criminal organization. The Crimson Lotus syndicate is known for being ruthless killers and a menace to the otherwise safe streets of Seoul.

Their origins started long before people started fleeing North Korea. Based on the extensive file the military keeps they have ties to an old-world order associated with the Han dynasty. *How could his sister get mixed up with these people?*

I don't know for sure if it's a match but I keep looking at the associated images for her profile. I stop scrolling and stop at a picture that is familiar. It's the same picture I remember seeing in Jun Pyo's car from the first night he gave me a ride home. The photo is a part of an article with the headline "Treason" in large black print at the top of the page.

I trace my index finger along the screen of my laptop reading the article.

While it's unclear when Jae Pyo will be released, there has been a motion for his release on behalf of his wife. Jae Pyo will have to appear before the courts. His family is expected to testify against him or could face the same punishment for his crimes. His article written two months ago mentioned criticizing government officials in the response to nuclear threats being presented from other countries. Currently Jae Pyo has a wife and two children, one currently presumed to be missing since his conviction. The end of the article mentions how treason of any kind will not be tolerated.

*Bingo, I say softly saving the profile of Suni in my system. There's the key to proving his connection... the sister.*

I call Dak and fill him in on the intel I found. There's not enough to prove Violetta's innocence but this is at least enough for Jun Pyo to get investigated. *He won't know what hit him.*

***

The sunlight peeks through the blinds as I lay down with my arms to my sides staring up at the vaulted ceiling. I hear my alarm going off on the nightstand. Hitting the STOP button my arm tenses from the motion.

I lay back down thinking about how this day will play out. It feels like a day of reckoning. Every memory I recall has been tainted with images of Jun Pyo leaking into my brain. *All I can do is think why couldn't I see him for who he really was?*

After countless minutes of thinking I know my brain needs a break and swing my legs over the side of the bed. The only way to quiet and clear my mind right now is through physical exercise. My morning run will be the escape I need.

Opening the door to my wardrobe I search through my dresser to find a pink workout suit. With my workout clothes in hand, I reach for a sports bra and underwear walking downstairs to the bathroom. I find solace that in just a few moments I can run and temporarily not think about what's to come.

*7:45 am DAK:* Do you have everything?

*7:47 am ME:* Yes, all set meet me here at my place

I text Dak as I walk back towards my apartment building. Bypassing a strange-looking man who holds the door for me, he has a cap pulled low over his eyes and looking down at his waist I can see he has a gun. I find it strange since carrying a gun is illegal in Seoul. Fighting the urge to observe I walk to the elevator.

Wanting to shower before Dak gets here, I round the corner and am surprised to see the door to my apartment is wide open. *What the hell?* I scan the hallway looking for signs of anyone but it's empty. I close the door quickly, not paying attention to anything, my only focus is on getting upstairs.

Running up the steps two at a time I reach the landing and see my work leather bag on top of the white comforter on my bed. An aching feeling plagues me as I lift it up feeling its weight. It's surprisingly light and even though I already know the reason, I open the top strap to find the bag empty. The burner phone and my laptop have disappeared. Tossing it down, my feelings sink with it to the floor. Feeling frustrated and unsure of what to do next I stare at the empty bag.

My nostrils flare in anger and looking for the closest thing I can destroy I grab my phone. I fling it hard to the ground. It feels good. The phone bounces back up and forcefully lands face down. My protective case is stronger than I thought as I pick up the phone and see no hint of damage.

With my mind racing I keep pacing between my bed and wardrobe closet. Getting more upset by the minute my shoes squeak on the wood floor. I hear knocking at the door and reach for my luger baseball bat I keep next to my nightstand.

Ready for anything I walk down the stairs. Reaching the door, I peer through the peephole with my left eye. A sigh of relief escapes, it's Dak. Placing the baseball bat down, I unlock the door.

"I thought you would meet me downstairs. I called, but you weren't answering," he says swiftly. His face stares down at my attire in the pink track suit.

"I'm sorry," I say, ushering him into the living room quickly.

"What's going on Mav? I mean look at this place," he gestures pointing a finger at the current state of the small space.

Ignoring his questions, I suspiciously ask. "Did anyone else know about our plan? What about Darcelle or Violetta?"

"No Mav, I just told them we found some information that could help. What's with the twenty-one questions and why does your place look like this?" he asks again.

"Someone broke into my apartment... my laptop is gone and the burner phone."

"Seriously... bloody hell, you can still access the file from the office. Right?

*I can... I should,* letting out a breath of air loudly I try to convince myself we can still do this. I just can't believe someone would break into this place. *How would they even know we're on to something?* Finishing my short rant my eyes brim with tears wanting to spill out.

Dak walks towards me and grabs my arm lightly.

"Maverick, these people are dangerous and that's why we have to expose them. Let me clean up this stuff. You get dressed so we can leave."

Nodding my head up and down I inspect my apartment surveying the damage done. The couch has a huge slash on the back and side. A silver lamp I bought from the first night I saw Jun Pyo at the home goods store lays on the floor in pieces and the spare computer monitor I have at a small desk near the door appears to be destroyed. I had been so preoccupied with going upstairs I failed to see just how much had been misplaced.

After thanking Dak for his help, I take one last look at my ravaged living room and head upstairs. Preparing myself for a fight I grab my leather pencil skirt, red button-down shirt, and my black stiletto pumps.

*It's war they'll get.*

# Chapter 20

Dressed to kill, I smooth over my skirt and tuck one long braid behind my ear. I apply a light layer of red matte lip gloss to my lips. Dak navigates smoothly through the heavy morning traffic towards the office. On the outside, I appear calm, controlled, and unfazed but my insides tell a different story. A bundle of nerves in my stomach and a scorned heart weighing heavier than the Titanic. Although I'm physically in the car my head is stuck in the past.

Visions of Jun Pyo flood my mind. What I took for a chance at love was calculated deceit. Coming back to the present I stare out the window. Hearing Dak mention taking a shortcut he sharply merges in the far-left lane turning on a side street. I continue staring aimlessly but at the sight of a familiar place I sit up in my seat. We drive past the Koi Fish bar; from the night I apologized to Jun Pyo. It seems foolish but I pull out my phone and my thumb hovers over Jun Pyo's contact number.

I wish he would have been honest or just let me out of whatever plot he had going on. Instead of listening to my heart which tells me to call and see if this is some sick joke, I listen to my brain and lock my phone not ready to delete his phone number. The rest of the ride to the office is a blur. Now is the moment to put it all on the line.

The American flag waves lightly in the air next to the Korean flag much like my mind clouds scatter making it appear gray outside. I look up to the sky praying for victory even if it is just for revenge. I have a hard time believing my prayer will be answered.

My thoughts are interrupted by the halt of the car. Dak is already standing outside the rear passenger door where I'm seated. His signature black suit hangs loosely as his body is still healing and doesn't look as muscular. He waits there holding the car door open for me waiting to step out. *Now or never.*

Holding my head high, I saunter into the grand double doors on the eleventh floor. The grand entryway seems intimidating as I hesitate to get off the elevator. Before proceeding into the office, I scan my badge and walk past the receptionist's desk. Greeted with a warm smile that I can't seem to return ,instead I nod my head slowly.

Walking towards my desk my steps are interrupted by someone calling my name. My head swivels around to see who is calling me.

Eun Ji appears before me. I mentally prepare myself for a smart remark from her and look at her top to bottom her signature red lips are pursed so thin against her mouth, and the gray wrap dress hugs her small frame. Only in this instance does she look innocent.

"Well look whose finally back from medical leave."

"Eun Ji," I say interrupting her. "Listen, whatever you're about to say, don't."

"Maverick, I was just welcoming you back… I mean Jun Pyo did tell me you took some time because of your incident." She feigns fake concerns and smirks at me.

*I want to wipe that thin-lipped smirk right off her face.*

Not allowing her to waste any more of my time I resume walking towards my office pushing her voice out of my ears. But not before she says, "Agent Choy might as well share your office with you."

My eyes are unnervingly wild making me look like a mad woman. It takes every ounce within me not to curse her ass out. My hand pushes the office door open. It seems weirdly empty like I was never even there even though I've only been gone a week.

Staring out the window behind my desk I recall first stepping into the office. *My* office. The wooden desk, the bookcase, and chaise chair seemed to take up so much space. But not even these pieces of furniture can remove the stale feeling I have. I walk behind my desk and sit down in the plush leather chair leaning my head back on the winged back chair. I crack my knuckles a bit and log on to my desktop computer hoping for a miracle.

The computer screen comes to life, and I'm prompted to log on after clicking a few keys on the keypad the computer starts loading. Every second feels like a minute as I follow my normal routine to access files. I click on my recent history, but nothing shows. I try another approach and type Jun Pyo's sister's name into the search bar. Unlike earlier when I located her file, now it says, "No file found" and I swear I hear my heart palpitate. *That can't be right.*

I type her name in again, slowly mouthing each letter silently, but it still says no file found. Not ready to give up yet I try one more search this time typing in Jun Pyo's father's name. His file appears easily, and my body instantly relaxes. I click desperately on his name but a yellow warning sign flashes. "CAUTION" it says simply. I click on the icon and in bold black letters it reads "This file is above your clearance."

A few links load after I continue accessing the file. The first link available is the article I first read about Jun Pyo's father being found guilty of treason. The article is the same one from before but where words were once, there are black marks redacting whatever I thought I found.

That sinking feeling returns, and nothing seems to get rid of it. *I have nothing. No physical proof. No one. No article. No laptop. NOTHING!* Closing my eyes and pinching the bridge of my nose an internal war within me plays out. *Should I even expose him? Who would believe me?*

A knock at the door ceases my thoughts. The cheery receptionist enters, not even waiting for my response to invite her in. She hastily says, "Colonel Davis would like to see you."

"Thank you, I'll be there shortly. I'm working on something," I say curtly hoping she gets the hint to leave.

"He wasn't really asking."

She looks on awkwardly waiting for me in the doorway.

I get up from my desk quickly and follow her while trying to think of a way that I can prove what I discovered. The receptionist leads the way and instead of making a right towards the colonel's office we make a left headed to the board rooms.

As we approach, I can see a few other legs under the see-through glass mirrored walls. We stop short of the door and I almost crash into the receptionist; her blonde hair is just inches away from my nose. She swiftly turns around backing up slightly.

"Well, good luck," then walks away.

I wait behind the door for a moment. Gathering my composure, I walk into the board room. I feel like I've interrupted some funny joke as I see Colonel Davis, Agent Choy, and Jun Pyo? They laugh sitting across from each other at the large table.

"Maverick, nice to see you," I hear Choy say meekly, the smile replaced with a nervous frown. She sits directly across from Jun Pyo who hasn't said a word. He only stares as I walk close next to the chair directly next to him, it's the only one available.

"Welcome back, Lieutenant Robinson. Let's get started with some recent changes," Colonel Davis belts out loudly leaving me little time for questions. I slide my chair closer to the wood table with my hands resting on top of each other.

Colonel Davis starts. "Maverick, this meeting is for some changes I deem necessary. Effective immediately you and Agent Choy will be co-chairing the department. As a result of the gala failure, I feel collectively that you may need more time to..." he pauses, "get used to how we do things here." He stops gauging my response.

I can't say anything. I stare aimlessly while looking at the way his vein thumps. I feel a slight touch on my thigh, it's Jun Pyo. It appears everyone is staring at me now. I place my right hand under the table quickly and shoot daggers letting him know not to touch me.

Instead, his eyes plead for me to be present. He shifts his eyes between me and back to Colonel Davis. For a moment I consider the plan to expose him could be called off, but I know in my heart this isn't possible. *I can't live in my lies or other peoples' anymore... not anymore.*

I'm doing my best not to feel the heat from his touch radiating as everyone waits for me to speak.

"I understand the gala event was a disappointment but I feel I'm qualified to run this team. I, along with some others believe the gala along with a string of other assignments have been compromised by someone in this room," I say staring directly at Colonel Davis.

He interrupts— "What do you mean compromised? Is this more of that gossip crap? I thought I told you to leave it alone," he says sternly. The vein in his neck looks like it's about pop out from under his skin.

"It's not a rumor. I have reason to believe Violetta Stone was framed in multiple cases. We found a pattern and believe Agent Jun Pyo could be aiding the same people that compromised the gala event."

A small gasp escapes Agent Choy's mouth and she places her hand over her lips. I just can't seem to look over, but I feel that familiar pressure of knowing his gaze is on me.

Forcing myself to continue speaking "I located some files indicating Jun---I mean Agent Pyo is the common factor in a string of failed surveillances. He also has a personal relationship to Crimson Lotus Syndicate with a high level ranking member." The words spill out of me rushed and unorganized and the silence in the room is eerie.

Colonel Davis' eyes bounce between Jun Pyo and I. He silently weighs what I've just said.

"Do you have any proof to validate anything you're saying?"

"Umm, we did, I mean there were some files confirming the connections, but they have been redacted. But I can prove--

"Enough!" he screams. "You know this department doesn't need any more gossip or scandal. You've worked with this man—he's the only person that even recommended you continue running this team. And who is this 'we' you keep referring to?"

Instead of responding, I finally build the courage to look over at Jun Pyo. His face seems unreadable but after learning his body and expressions I can tell he's angry—no sad? His eyes blaze an inferno and it's all directed at me.

"Robinson, answer now!" Colonel Davis slaps his hand on the table filling the conference room with an echo.

Clearing my throat multiple times but still looking at Jun Pyo. *What did he mean he's the only one that wanted me here? How could that even be true, he's a liar, the worst type that uses people. Doing nice things that make you second guess his intentions.*

"Umm I—ahem, mentioned my concerns to another colleague and he gave me more details on how things worked when Stone was here. Darcelle also shared some concerning details that---"

"Just stop. You talked to Darccelle Ramirez? Ramirez, the same woman we assumed helped contribute to the gala attack? The woman that's aligned with a suspected terrorist? You can't be serious."

"I didn't—" I start to finish but Colonel Davis raises his finger silencing me.

"You're done," he says simply. "I think you've embarrassed this department and the service enough and I will have you investigated. If you had anything to do with sharing high-level government information trust me, you will regret it. You're dismissed and expected to report back home immediately."

The tears well up in my eyes and it hits me that he's serious. I feel like a prisoner that wants to plead his case. My mouth opens and closes the sinking feelings I've tried to keep at bay emerge. Looking over one last time at the cause of my heartache I see the slightest twitch from Jun Pyo's mouth but his stone features return in an instant and he sits there not defending or even discrediting anything I've said. I mouth the words "coward" and exit the boardroom quickly before anyone can stop me.

The embarrassment clouds whatever rational thoughts should be directing me scrambling to the women's restroom. I open the door so hard this it hits the wall making a wicked noise. I close the door a little more gently and lock it.

Staring in the mirror the person staring back at me isn't a grown woman it's HER. The girl who gave up on herself and love so long ago. She believes in a savior that ceases to exist in her mind. The only thing this version of herself believes is that she deserves every bad thing that's ever happened to her. It's a payment she must pay for the rest of her life.

The dark thoughts I always try to subside creep in. *You were never good enough for this job anyway. You're good at keeping your mouth shut, just like before. You can't even stand up for yourself. You thought he liked you, he played because you allowed him to. You're not good at relationships so why would this have been any different? Who falls in love with a man that's a mystery? Did you really think anyone would believe you... you? I guess this will be another skeleton you put in our closet.*

My tears coat my face and any hint of makeup I previously applied to my face has somehow become smudged from the tears and wiping of my face. My vision becomes blurred, and I continue staring back at myself. Not caring about the snot dripping from my nose I can't draw my eyes away from the way my face looks. Staring at the mirror is like taking a glimpse into my soul. The parts of me I never forgave for allowing others to make choices for me, to be treated like a game. The darkest parts of me somehow are revealed under the fluorescent lights of the bathroom.

My evil twin laughs maliciously pointing back at the frail, powerless version of the real me.

*And to think you had feelings for him. He just used you. Mom is going to lose her shit about this one,* my reflection says and keeps laughing.

My last point of resolve snaps and I punch the mirror. An excruciating pain cripples my tears. Turning towards the door before I look at the damage I've done there's a low knock. For some reason I already know it's him.

Looking back at the mirror I see a small crack. Mirror one, me zero. Other than a small fleck of a crack there isn't much damage. My evil twin seems to have retreated as well. I rub my right hand softly feeling the tenderness around my knuckle from the punch.

I continue hearing the knock, inching closer to him... I mean the door. He calls my name.

"Maverick, please come out." He isn't screaming but his voice is loud enough to be heard through the thick door.

With my back against the wall of the door I breathe out, "You lied to me." My voice cracks and is so low I find it hard to believe he even heard me.

He calls my name again a little louder. Placing my hand on the lock, I twist it to the left and hear a click. With my weight still forcing the door shut he slides in between the small space available. Easing in past me he looks under the stalls making sure no one else is here.

"You shouldn't be in here, let alone be anywhere near me." I want to sound upset but I can tell I sound defeated.

"That's not important---" he stutters his next words out quickly, "I'm sorry." The space between us gets closed in seconds.

His arms wrap around me and for a moment I push him away, but my efforts are no competition for his strength. I should fight back harder but inhaling his scent brings me comfort. His right hand runs over my face repeatedly and then my nose, until finally settling on my chin.

Our eyes are locked into some trance of one another and even though I'm in his arms my face still reads unimaginable anger.

All he says is, "You weren't supposed to find out like this."

**THE END**

# About the Author

Crystal Symone Crystal Symone is a poet, writer, and book enthusiast. Born and raised in North Carolina. She started writing poetry in middle school and throughout her college years. Writing poetry is her first love she enjoys writing short stories and essays about the African American experience of young women.

Crystal hopes to inspire others to express themselves and provide knowledge she's gained along her own personal journey. She enjoys being a creative writer and helping those in her community.

For more books by Crystal visit her website

*authorcrystalsymone. com*

If you or someone you know is contemplating motherhood and is weighing the possibility of having an abortion, call 1-800-712-HELP (4357).